The King of Ireland's Son

The King
of Ireland's Son

Padraic Colum
Illustrated by Willy Pogany

Floris Classics

First published in 1916 by the Macmillan Company
Fourth edition published in 1986 by Floris Books
Reprinted in 1997

British Library CIP Data available

Colum, Padraic
The King of Ireland's son: an Irish folk tale
— 4th ed.
1. children's stories
I. Title
823'.912[J]   PZ7

ISBN 0-86315-512-X

Printed in Great Britain
by Page Bros (Norwich) Ltd

CONTENTS

Fedelma the Enchanter's Daughter   2

When the King of the Cats Came to King Connal's Dominion   52

The Sword of Light and the Unique Tale, With as Much of the Adventures of Gilly of the Goatskin as is Given in "The Craneskin Book"   80

The Town of the Red Castle   161

The King of the Land of Mist   194

The House of Crom Duv   211

The Spae-Woman   255

ILLUSTRATIONS

The King of Ireland's Son quickly gathered them
into his bag   *20*

The creature caught him in its long arms   *82*

"Oh, if that's a hazel rod he has at his bow he will
kill us all!"   *100*

He rode on a bob-tailed, big-headed, spavined, and
spotted horse   *115*

She saw the corpse sitting up stiffly   *140*

Then a maiden came   *163*

Flame-of-Wine laughed with mockery   *191*

Flann was dragged on   *216*

Up it came, a great black horse with a sweeping
mane   *247*

FEDELMA THE
ENCHANTER'S DAUGHTER

I

CONNAL was the name of the King who ruled over Ireland at that time. He had three sons, and, as the fir trees grow, some crooked and some straight, one of them grew up so wild that in the end the King and the King's Councillor had to let him have his own way in everything. This youth was the King's eldest son and his mother had died before she could be a guide to him.

Now after the King and the King's Councillor left him to his own way the youth I'm telling you about did nothing but ride and hunt all day. Well, one morning he rode abroad—

> His hound at his heel,
> His hawk on his wrist;
> A brave steed to carry him whither he list,
> And the blue sky over him,

and he rode on until he came to a turn in the road. There he saw a gray old man seated on a heap of stones playing a game of cards with himself. First he had one hand winning and then he had the other. Now he would say "That's my good right," and then he would say "Play and beat that, my gallant left." The King of Ireland's Son sat on his horse to watch the strange old man, and as he watched him he sang a song to himself—

> I put the fastenings on my boat
>   For a year and for a day,
> And I went where the rowans grow,
>   And where the moorhens lay;
>
> And I went over the steppingstones
>   And dipped my feet in the ford,
> And came at last to the Swineherd's house—
>   The Youth without a Sword.
>
> A swallow sang upon his porch
>   "Glu-ee, glu-ee, glu-ee,"
> "The wonder of all wandering,
>   The wonder of the sea";
> A swallow soon to leave ground sang
>   "Glu-ee, glu-ee, glu-ee."

"Prince," said the old fellow looking up at him, "if you can play a game as well as you can sing a song, I'd like if you would sit down beside me."

"I can play any game," said the King of Ireland's Son. He fastened his horse to the branch of a tree and sat down on the heap of stones beside the old man.

"What shall we play for?" said the gray old fellow.

"Whatever you like," said the King of Ireland's Son.

"If I win you must give me anything I ask, and if you win I shall give you anything you ask. Will you agree to that?"

"If it is agreeable to you it is agreeable to me," said the King of Ireland's Son.

They played, and the King of Ireland's Son won the game. "Now what do you desire me to give, King's Son?" said the gray old fellow.

"I shan't ask you for anything," said the King of Ireland's Son, "for I think you haven't much to give."

"Never mind that," said the gray old fellow. "I mustn't break my promise, and so you must ask me for something."

"Very well," said the King's Son. "Then there's a field at the back of my father's Castle and I want to see it filled with cattle tomorrow morning. Can you do that for me?"

"I can," said the gray old fellow.

"Then I want fifty cows, each one white with a red ear, and a white calf going beside each cow."

"The cattle shall be as you wish."

"Well, when that's done I shall think the wager has been paid," said the King of Ireland's Son. He mounted his horse, smiling at the foolish old man who played cards with himself and who thought he could bring together fifty white kine, each with a red ear, and a white calf by the side of each cow. He rode away—

> His hound at his heel,
> His hawk on his wrist;
> A brave steed to carry him whither he list,
> And the green ground under him,

and he thought no more of the gray old fellow.

But in the morning, when he was taking his horse out of the stable, he heard the grooms talking about a strange happening. Art, the King's Steward, had gone out and had found the field at the back of the Castle filled with cattle. There were fifty white red-eared kine there and each cow had a white calf at her side. The King had ordered Art, his Steward, to drive them away. The King of Ireland's Son watched Art and his men trying to do it. But no sooner were the strange cattle put out at one side of the field than they came back on the other. Then down came Maravaun, the King's Councillor. He declared they were enchanted cattle, and that no one on Ireland's ground could put them away. So in the seven-acre field the cattle stayed.

When the King of Ireland's Son saw what his companion of yesterday could do he rode straight to the glen to try if he could have another game with him. There at the turn of the road, on a heap of stones, the gray old fellow was sitting playing a game of cards, the right hand against the left. The King of Ireland's Son fastened his horse to the branch of a tree and dismounted.

"Did you find yesterday's wager settled?" said the gray old fellow.

"I did," said the King of Ireland's Son.

"Then shall we have another game of cards on the same understanding?" said the gray old fellow.

"I agree, if you agree," said the King of Ireland's Son. He sat under the bush beside him and they played again. The King of Ireland's Son won.

"What would you like me to do for you this time?" said the gray old fellow.

Now the King's Son had a stepmother, and she was often cross-tempered, and that very morning he and she had vexed each other. So he said, "Let a brown bear, holding a burning coal in his mouth, put Caintigern the Queen from her chair in the supper room tonight."

"It shall be done," said the gray old fellow.

Then the King of Ireland's Son mounted his horse and rode away—

> His hound at his heel,
> His hawk on his wrist;
> A brave steed to carry him whither he list,
> And the green ground under him,

and he went back to the Castle. That night a brown bear, holding a burning coal in his mouth, came into the supper room and stood between Caintigern the Queen and the chair that belonged to her. None of the servants could drive it away, and when Maravaun, the King's Councillor, came he said, "This is an enchanted creature also, and it is best for us to leave it alone." So the whole company went and left the brown bear in the supper room seated in the Queen's chair.

II

THE next morning when he wakened the King's Son said, "That was a wonderful thing that happened last night in the supper room. I must go off and play a third game with the gray old fellow who sits on a heap of stones at the turn of the road." So, in the morning early he mounted and rode away—

> His hound at his heel,
> His hawk on his wrist;
> A brave steed to carry him whither he list,
> And the green ground under him,

and he rode on until he came to the turn in the road. Sure enough the old gray fellow was there. "So you've come to me again, King's Son," said he. "I have," said the King of Ireland's Son, "and I'll play a last game with you on the same understanding as before." He tied his horse to the branch and sat down on the heap of stones. They played. The King of Ireland's Son lost the game. Immediately the gray old fellow threw the cards down on the stones and a wind came up and carried them away. Standing up he was terribly tall.

"King's Son," said he, "I am your father's enemy and I have done him an injury. And to the Queen who is your father's wife I have done an injury too. You have lost the game and now you must take the penalty I put upon you. You must find out my dwelling place and take three hairs out of my beard within a year and a day, or else lose your head."

With that he took the King of Ireland's Son by the shoulders and lifted him on his horse, turning the horse in the direction of the King's Castle. The King's Son rode on—

· 7 ·

His hound at his heel,
His hawk on his wrist;
A brave steed to carry him whither he list,
And the blue sky over him.

That evening the King noticed that his son was greatly troubled. And when he lay down to sleep everyone in the Castle heard his groans and his moans. The next day he told his father the story from beginning to end. The King sent for Maravaun his Councillor and asked him if he knew who the Enchanter was and where his son would be likely to find him.

"From what he said," said Maravaun, "we may guess who he is. He is the Enchanter of the Black Back-Lands and his dwelling place is hard to find. Nevertheless your son must seek for him and take the three hairs out of his beard or else lose his head. For if the heir to your kingdom does not honorably pay his forfeit, the ground of Ireland won't give crops and the cattle won't give milk." "And," said the Councillor, "as a year is little for his search, he should start off at once, although I'm bound to say, that I don't know what direction he should go in."

The next day the King's Son said goodby to his father and his foster brothers and started off on his journey. His stepmother would not give him her blessing on account of his having brought in the brown bear that turned her from her chair in the supper room. Nor would she let him have the good horse he always rode. Instead the Prince was given a horse that was lame in a leg and short in the tail. And neither hawk nor hound went with him this time.

All day the King's Son was going, traveling through wood and waste until the coming on of night. The little fluttering birds were going from the bush tops, from tuft to tuft, and to the briar-roots, going to rest; but if they were, he was not, till the night came on, blind and dark. Then the King's Son ate his bread and meat, put his satchel under his head and lay down to take his rest on the edge of a great waste.

In the morning he mounted his horse and rode on. And as he went across the waste he saw an extraordinary sight—everywhere were the bodies of dead creatures— a cock, a wren, a mouse, a weasel, a fox, a badger, a raven —all the birds and beasts that the King's Son had ever known. He went on, but he saw no living creature before him. And then, at the end of the waste he came upon two living creatures· struggling. One was an eagle and the other was an eel. And the eel had twisted itself round the eagle, and the eagle had covered her eyes with the black films of death. The King's Son jumped off his horse and cut the eel in two with a sharp stroke of his sword.

The eagle drew the films from her eyes and looked full at the King's Son. "I am Laheen the Eagle," she said, "and I will pay you for this service, Son of King Connal. Know that there has been a battle of the creatures—a battle to decide which of the creatures will make laws for a year. All were killed except the eel and myself, and if you had not come I would have been killed and the eel would have made the laws. I am Laheen the Eagle and always I will be your friend. And now you must tell me how I can serve you."

"You can serve me," said the King's Son, "by showing me how I may come to the dominion of the Enchanter of the Black Back-Lands."

"I am the only creature who can show you, King's Son. And if I were not old now I would carry you there on my back. But I can tell you how you can get there. Ride forward for a day, first with the sun before you and then with the sun at your back, until you come to the shore of a lake. Stay there until you see three swans flying down. They are the three daughters of the Enchanter of the Black Back-Lands. Mark the one who carries a green scarf in her mouth. She is the youngest daughter and the one who can help you. When the swans come to the ground they will transform themselves into maidens and bathe in the lake. Two will come out, put on their swanskins and transform themselves and fly away. But you must hide the swanskin that belongs to the youngest maiden. She will search and search and when she cannot find it she will cry out, 'I would do anything in the world for the creature who would find my swanskin for me.' Give the swanskin to her then, and tell her that the only thing she can do for you is to show you the way to her father's dominion. She will do that, and so you will come to the House of the Enchanter of the Black Back-Lands. And now farewell to you, Son of King Connal."

Laheen the Eagle spread out her wings and flew away, and the King's Son journeyed on, first with the sun before him and then with the sun at his back, until he came to the shore of a wide lake. He turned his horse away, rested himself on the ground, and as soon as the clear day came he began to watch for the three swans.

III

THEY came, they flew down, and when they touched the ground they transformed themselves into three maidens and went to bathe in the lake. The one who carried the green scarf left her swanskin under a bush. The King's Son took it and hid it in a hollow tree.

Two of the maidens soon came out of the water, put on their swanskins and flew away as swans. The younger maiden stayed for a while in the lake. Then she came out and began to search for her swanskin. She searched and searched, and at last the King's Son heard her say, "I would do anything in the world for the creature who would find my swanskin for me." Then he came from where he was hiding and gave her the swanskin. "I am the Son of the King of Ireland," he said, "and I want you to show me the way to your father's dominion."

"I would prefer to do anything else for you," said the maiden.

"I do not want anything else," said the King of Ireland's Son.

"If I show you how to get there will you be content?"

"I shall be content."

"You must never let my father know that I showed you the way. And he must not know when you come that you are the King of Ireland's Son."

"I will not tell him you showed me the way and I will not let him know who I am."

Now that she had the swanskin she was able to transform herself. She whistled and a blue falcon came down and perched on a tree. "That falcon is my own bird," said she. "Follow where it flies and you will come to my father's house. And now goodby to you. You will be in danger, but I will try to help you. Fedelma is my name." She rose up as a swan and flew away.

The blue falcon went flying from bush to bush and from rock to rock. The night came, but in the morning the blue falcon was seen again. The King's Son followed, and at last he saw a house before him. He went in, and there, seated on a chair of gold was the man who seemed so tall when he threw down the cards upon the heap of stones. The Enchanter did not recognize the King's Son without his hawk and his hound and the fine clothes he used to wear. He asked who he was and the King's Son said he was a youth who had just finished an apprenticeship to a wizard. "And," said he, "I have heard that you have three fair daughters, and I came to strive to gain one of them for a wife."

"In that case," said the Enchanter of the Black Back-

Lands, "you will have to do three tasks for me. If you
are able to do them I will give you one of my three
daughters in marriage. If you fail to do any one of them
you will lose your head. Are you willing to make the
trial?"

"I am willing," said the King of Ireland's Son.

"Then I shall give you your first task tomorrow. It
is unlucky that you came today. In this country we eat
a meal only once a week, and we have had our meal
this morning."

"It is all the same to me," said the King's Son, "I can
do without food or drink for a month without any hard-
ship."

"I suppose you can do without sleep too?" said the
Enchanter of the Black Back-Lands.

"Easily," said the King of Ireland's Son.

"That is good. Come outside now, and I'll show you
your bed." He took the King's Son outside and showed
him a dry narrow watertank at the gable end of the house.
"There is where you are to sleep," said the Enchanter.
"Tuck yourself into it now and be ready for your first
task at the rising of the sun."

The King of Ireland's Son went into the little tank.
He was uncomfortable there you may be sure. But in
the middle of the night Fedelma came and brought him
into a fine room where he ate and then slept until the
sun was about to rise in the morning. She called him
and he went outside and laid himself down in the watertank.

As soon as the sun rose the Enchanter of the Black Back-Lands came out of the house and stood beside the watertank. "Come now," said he, "and I will show you the first task you have to perform." He took him to where a herd of goats was grazing. Away from the goats was a fawn with white feet and little bright horns. The fawn saw them, bounded into the air, and raced away to the wood as quickly as any arrow that a man ever shot from a bow.

"That is Whitefoot the Fawn," said the Enchanter of the Black Back-Lands. "She grazes with my goats but none of my gillies can bring her into my goathouse. Here is your first task—run down Whitefoot the Fawn and bring her with my goats into the goat shelter this evening." When he said that the Enchanter of the Black Back-Lands went away laughing to himself.

"Goodby, my life," said the King of Ireland's Son, "I might as well try to catch an eagle on the wing as to run down the deer that has gone out of sight already."

He sat down on the ground and his despair was great. Then his name was called and he saw Fedelma coming toward him. She looked at him as though she were in dread. and said, "What task has my father set you?" He told her and then she smiled. "I was in dread it would be a more terrible task," she said. "This one is easy. I can help you to catch Whitefoot the Fawn. But first eat what I have brought you."

She put down bread and meat and wine, and they sat

down and he ate and drank. "I thought he might set you this task," she said, "and so I brought you something from my father's store of enchanted things. Here are the Shoes of Swiftness. With these on your feet you can run down Whitefoot the Fawn. But you must catch her before she has gone very far away. Remember that she must be brought in when the goats are going into their shelter at sunset. You will have to walk back for all the time you must keep hold of her silver horns. Hasten now. Run her down with the Shoes of Swiftness and then lay hold of her horns. Above all things Whitefoot dreads the loss of her silver horns."

He thanked Fedelma. He put on the Shoes of Swiftness and went into the wood. Now he could go as the eagle flies. He found Whitefoot the Fawn drinking at the Raven's pool.

When she saw him she went from thicket to thicket. The Shoes of Swiftness were hardly any use to him in these shut-in places. At last he beat her from the last thicket. It was the hour of noontide then. There was a clear plain before them and with the Shoes of Swiftness he ran her down. There were tears in the Fawn's eyes and he knew she was troubled with the dread of losing her silver horns.

He kept his hands on the horns and they went back over miles of plain and pasture, bog and wood. The hours were going quicker than they were going. When he came within the domain of the Enchanter of the Black Back-Lands he saw the goats going quickly before him.

They were hurrying from their pastures to the goat shelter, one stopping, maybe, to bite the top of a hedge and another giving this one a blow with her horns to hurry her on. "By your silver horns, we must go faster," said the King of Ireland's Son to the Fawn. They went more quickly then.

He saw the Enchanter of the Black Back-Lands waiting at the goathouse, now counting the goats that came along and now looking at the sun. When he saw the King of Ireland's Son coming with his capture he was so angry that he struck an old full-bearded goat that had stopped to rub itself. The goat reared up and struck him with his horns.

"Well," said the Enchanter of the Black Back-Lands, "you have performed your first task, I see. You are a greater enchanter than I thought you were. Whitefoot the Fawn can go in with my goats. Go back now to your own sleeping place. Tomorrow I'll come to you early and give you your second task."

The King of Ireland's Son went back and into the dry watertank. He was tired with his day's journey after Whitefoot the Fawn. It was his hope that Fedelma would come to him and give him shelter for that night.

IV

UNTIL the white moon rose above the trees; until the hounds went out hunting for themselves; until the foxes came down and hid in the hedges, waiting for the cocks and hens to stir out at the first light—so long did the King of Ireland's Son stay huddled in the dry watertank.

By that time he was stiff and sore and hungry. He saw a great white owl flying toward the tank. The owl perched on the edge and stared at the King's Son. "Have you a message for me?" he asked. The owl shrugged with its wings three times. He thought that meant a message. He got out of the tank and prepared to follow the owl. It flew slowly and near the ground, so he was able to follow it along a path through the wood.

The King's Son thought the owl was bringing him to a place where Fedelma was, and that he would get food there, and shelter for the rest of the night. And sure enough the owl flew to a little house in the wood. The King's Son looked through the window and he saw a room lighted with candles and a table with plates and dishes and cups, with bread and meat and wine. And he saw at the fire a young woman spinning at a spinning wheel, and her back was toward him, and her hair was the same as Fedelma's. Then he lifted the latch of the door and went very joyfully into the little house.

But when the young woman at the spinning wheel turned round he saw that she was not Fedelma at all. She had a little mouth, a long and a hooked nose, and her eyes looked cross-ways at a person. The thread she was spinning she bit with her long teeth, and she said, "You are welcome here, Prince."

"And who are you?" said the King of Ireland's Son.

"Aefa is my name," said she, "I am the eldest and the wisest daughter of the Enchanter of the Black Back-Lands.

My father is preparing a task for you," said she, "and it will be a terrible task, and there will be no one to help you with it, so you will lose your head surely. And what I would advise you to do is to escape out of this country at once."

"And how can I escape?" said the King of Ireland's Son.

"There's only one way to escape," said she, "and that is for you to take the Slight Red Steed that my father has secured under nine locks. That steed is the only creature that can bring you to your own country. I will show you how to get it and then I will ride to your home with you."

"And why should you do that?" said the King of Ireland's Son.

"Because I would marry you," said Aefa.

"But," said he, "if I live at all Fedelma is the one I will marry."

No sooner did he say the words than Aefa screamed out, "Seize him, my cat-o'-the-mountain. Seize him and hold him." Then the cat-o'-the-mountain that was under the table sprang across the room and fixed himself on his shoulder. He ran out of the house. All the time he was running the cat-o'-the-mountain was trying to tear his eyes out. He made his way through woods and thickets, and mighty glad he was when he saw the tank at the gable-end of the house. The cat-o'-the-mountain dropped from his back then. He got into the tank and waited and waited. No message came from Fedelma. He was a long time there, stiff and sore and hungry, before the sun rose and the Enchanter of the Black Back-Lands came out of the house.

V

I HOPE you had a good night's rest," said the Enchanter of of the Black Back-Lands, when he came to where the King of Ireland's Son was crouched, just at the rising of the sun. "I had indeed," said the King's Son. "And I suppose you feel fit for another task," said the Enchanter of the Black Back-Lands. "More fit than ever in my life before," said the King of Ireland's Son.

The Enchanter of the Black Back-Lands took him past the goathouse and to where there was an open shelter for his beehives. "I want this shelter thatched," said he, "and I want to have it thatched with the feathers of birds. Go," said he, "and get enough feathers of wild birds and come back and thatch the beehive shelter for me, and let it be done before the set of sun." He gave the King's Son arrows and a bow and a bag to put the feathers in, and advised him to search the moor for birds. Then he went back to the house.

The King of Ireland's Son ran to the moor and watched for birds to fly across. At last one came. He shot at it with an arrow but did not bring it down. He hunted the moor all over but found no other bird. He hoped that he would see Fedelma before his head was taken off.

Then he heard his name called and he saw Fedelma coming toward him. She looked at him as before with

*The King of Ireland's Son quickly
gathered them into his bag.*

dread in her eyes and asked him what task her father had set him. "A terrible task," he said, and he told her what it was. Fedelma laughed. "I was in dread he would give you another task," she said. "I can help you with this one. Sit down now and eat and drink from what I have brought you."

He sat down and ate and drank and he felt hopeful seeing Fedelma beside him. When he had eaten Fedelma said, "My blue falcon will gather the birds and pull the feathers off for you. Still, unless you gather them quickly there is danger, for the roof must be thatched with feathers at the set of sun." She whistled and her blue falcon came. He followed it across the moor. The blue falcon flew up in the air and gave a birdcall. Birds gathered and she swooped amongst them pulling feathers off their backs and out of their wings. Soon there was a heap of feathers on the ground—pigeons' feathers and pie's feathers, crane's and crow's, blackbird's and starling's. The King of Ireland's Son quickly gathered them into his bag. The falcon flew to another place and gave her birdcall again. The birds gathered, and she went amongst them, plucking their feathers. The King's Son gathered them and the blue falcon flew to another place. Over and over again the blue falcon called to the birds and plucked out their feathers, and over and over again the King's Son gathered them into his bag. When he thought he had feathers enough to thatch the roof he ran back to the shelter. He began the thatching, binding the feathers down with little willow rods. He had just finished when the sun went down. The old Enchanter came up and when he saw what the King's Son had done he was greatly surprised. "You surely learned from the wizard you were apprenticed to," said he. "But tomorrow I will try you with another task. Go now and sleep in the place where you were last night." The King's Son, glad that the head was still on his shoulders, went and lay down in the watertank.

VI

UNTIL the white moon went out in the sky; until the Secret People began to whisper in the woods—so long did the King of Ireland's Son remain in the dry watertank that night.

And then, when it was neither dark nor light, he saw a crane flying toward him. It lighted on the edge of the tank. "Have you a message for me?" said the King of Ireland's Son. The crane tapped three times with its beak. Then the King's Son got out of the tank and prepared to follow the bird-messenger.

This was the way the crane went. It would fly a little way and then light on the ground until the Prince came up to it. Then it would fly again. Over marshes and across little streams the crane led him. And all the time the King of Ireland's Son thought he was being brought to the place where Fedelma was—to the place where he would get food and where he could rest until just before the sun rose.

They went on and on till they came to an old tower. The crane lighted upon it. The King's Son saw there was an iron door in the tower and he pulled a chain until it opened. Then he saw a little room lighted with candles, and he saw a young woman looking at herself in the glass. Her back was toward him and her hair was the same as Fedelma's.

But when the young woman turned round he saw she was not Fedelma. She was little, and she had a face that was brown and tight like a nut. She made herself very friendly to the King of Ireland's Son and went to him and took his hands and smiled into his face.

"You are welcome here," said she.

"Who are you?" he asked.

"I am Gilveen," said she, "the second and the most loving of the three daughters of the Enchanter of the Black Back-Lands." She stroked his face and his hands when she spoke to him.

"And why did you send for me?"

"Because I know what great trouble you are in. My father is preparing a task for you, and it will be a terrible one. You will never be able to carry it out."

"And what should you advise me to do, King's daughter?"

"Let me help you. In this tower," said she, "there are the wisest books in the world. We'll surely find in one of them a way for you to get from this country. And then I'll go back with you to your own land."

"Why would you do that?" asked the King of Ireland's Son.

"Because I wish to be your wife," Gilveen said.

"But," said he, "if I live at all Fedelma is the one I'll marry."

When he said that Gilveen drew her lips together and her chin became like a horn. Then she whistled through her teeth, and instantly everything in the room began to attack the King's Son. The looking glass on the wall flung itself at him and hit him on the back of the head. The leg of the table gave him a terrible blow at the back of the knees. He saw the two candles hopping across the floor to burn his legs. He ran out of the room, and when he got to the door it swung around and gave him a blow that flung him away from the tower. The crane that was waiting on the tower flew down, its neck and beak outstretched, and gave him a blow on the back.

So the King of Ireland's Son went back over the marshes and across the little streams, and he was glad when he saw the gable-end of the house again.

He went into the tank. He knew that he had not long to wait before the sun would rise and the Enchanter of the Black Back-Lands would come to him and give him the third and the most difficult of the three tasks. And he thought that Fedelma was surely shut away from him and that she would not be able to help him that day.

VII

A T THE rising of the sun the Enchanter of the Black Back-Lands came to where the King of Ireland's Son was huddled and said, "I am now going to set you the third and last task. Rise up now and come with me."

The King's Son came out of the watertank and followed the Enchanter. They went to where there was a well.

The King's Son looked down and he could not see the bottom, so deep the well was. "At the bottom," said the Enchanter, "is the Ring of Youth. You must get it and bring it to me, or else you must lose your head at the setting of that sun." That was all he said. He turned then and went away.

The King's Son looked into the well and he saw no way of getting down its deep smooth sides. He walked back toward the Castle. On his way he met Fedelma, and she looked at him with deep dread in her eyes. "What task did my father set you today?" said she. "He bids me go down into a well," said, the King's Son. "A well!" said Fedelma, and she became all dread. "I have to take the Ring of Youth from the bottom and bring it to him," said the King's Son. "Oh," said Fedelma, "he has set you the task I dreaded."

Then she said, "You will lose your life if the Ring of Youth is not taken out of the well. And if you lose yours I shall lose my life too. There is one way to get down the sides of the well. You must kill me. Take my bones and make them as steps while you go down the sides. Then, when you have taken the Ring of Youth out of the water, put my bones as they were before, and put the Ring above my heart. I shall be alive again. But you must be careful that you leave every bone as it was."

The King's Son fell into a deeper dread than Fedelma when he heard what she said. "This can never be," he cried. "It must be," said she, "and by all your vows and promises I command that you do it. Kill me now and do as I have bidden you. If it be done I shall live. If it be not done you will lose your life and I will never regain mine."

He killed her. He took the bones as she had bidden him, and he made steps down the sides of the well. He searched at the bottom, and he found the Ring of Youth. He brought the bones together again. Down on his knees he went, and his heart did not beat nor did his breath come or go until he had fixed them in their places. Over the heart he placed the Ring. Life came back to Fedelma.

"You have done well," she said. "One thing only is not in its place—the joint of my little finger." She held up her hand and he saw that her little finger was bent.

"I have helped you in everything," said Fedelma, "and in the last task I could not have helped you if you had not been true to me when Aefa and Gilveen brought you to them. Now the three tasks are done, and you can ask my father for one of his daughters in marriage. When you bring him the Ring of Youth he will ask you to make a choice. I pray that the one chosen will be myself."

"None other will I have but you, Fedelma, love of my heart," said the King of Ireland's Son.

VIII

THE King of Ireland's Son went into the house before the setting of the sun. The Enchanter of the Black Back-Lands was seated on his chair of gold. "Have you brought me the Ring of Youth?" he asked.

"I have brought it," said the King's Son.

"Give it to me then," said the Enchanter.

"I will not," said the King's Son, "until you give what you promised me at the end of my tasks—one of your three daughters for my wife."

The Enchanter brought him to a closed door. "My three daughters are within that room," said he. "Put your hand through the hole in the door, and the one whose hand you hold when I open it—it is she you will have to marry."

Then wasn't the mind of the King's Son greatly troubled? If he held the hand of Aefa or Gilveen he would lose his love Fedelma. He stood without putting out his hand. "Put your hand through the hole of the door or go away from my house altogether," said the Enchanter of the Black Back-Lands.

The King of Ireland's Son ventured to put his hand through the hole in the door. The hands of the maidens inside were all held in a bunch. But no sooner did he touch them than he found that one had a broken finger. This he knew was Fedelma's hand, and this was the hand he held.

"You may open the door now," said he to the Enchanter.

He opened the door and the King of Ireland's Son drew Fedelma to him. "This is the maiden I choose," said he, "and now give her her dowry."

"The dowry that should go with me," said Fedelma, "is the Slight Red Steed."

"What dowry do you want with her, young man?" said the Enchanter.

"No other dowry but the Slight Red Steed."

"Go round to the stable then and get it. And I hope no well-trained wizard like you will come this way again."

"No well-trained wizard am I, but the King of Ireland's Son. And I have found your dwelling-place within a year and a day. And now I pluck the three hairs out of your beard, Enchanter of the Black Back-Lands."

The beard of the Enchanter bristled like spikes on a hedgehog, and the balls of his eyes stuck out of his head. The King's Son plucked the three hairs of his beard before he could lift a hand or say a word. "Mount the Slight Red Steed and be off, the two of you," said the Enchanter.

The King of Ireland's Son and Fedelma mounted the Slight Red Steed and rode off, and the Enchanter of the Black Back-Lands, and his two daughters, Aefa and Gilveen, in a rage watched them ride away.

IX

THEY crossed the River of the Ox, and went over the Mountain of the Fox and were in the Glen of the Badger before the sun rose. And there, at the foot of the Hill of Horns, they found an old man gathering dew from the grass.

"Could you tell us where we might find the Little Sage of the Mountain?" Fedelma asked the old man.

"I am the Little Sage of the Mountain," said he, "and what is it you want of me?"

"To betroth us for marriage," said Fedelma.

"I will do that. Come to my house, the pair of you. And as you are both young and better able to walk than I am it would be fitting to let me ride on your horse."

The King's Son and Fedelma got off and the Little Sage of the Mountain got on the Slight Red Steed. They took the path that went round the Hill of Horns. And at the other side of the hill they found a hut thatched with one great wing of a bird. The Little Sage got off the Slight Red Steed. "Now," said he, "you're both young, and I'm an old man and it would be fitting for you to do my day's work before you call upon me to do anything for you. Now would you," said he to the King of Ireland's Son, "take this spade in your hand and go into the garden and dig my potatoes for me? And would you," said he to Fedelma, "sit down at the quern-stone and grind the wheat for me?"

The King of Ireland's Son went into the garden and Fedelma sat at the quern-stone that was just outside the door; he dug and she ground while the Little Sage sat at the fire looking into a big book. And when Fedelma and the King's Son were tired with their labor he gave them a drink of buttermilk.

She made cakes out of the wheat she had ground and the King's Son washed the potatoes and the Little Sage boiled them and so they made their supper. Then the Little Sage of the Mountain melted lead and made two rings; and one ring he gave to Fedelma to give to the King's Son and one he gave to the King's Son to give to Fedelma. And when the rings were given he said, "You are betrothed for your marriage now."

They stayed with the Little Sage of the Mountain that night, and when the sun rose they left the house that was thatched with the great wing of a bird and they turned toward the Meadow of Brightness and the Wood of Shadows that were between them and the King of Ireland's domain. They rode on the Slight Red Steed, and the Little Sage of the Mountain went with them a part of the way. He seemed downcast and when they asked him the reason he said, "I see dividing ways and far journeys for you both." "But how can that be," said the King's Son, "when, in a little while we will win to my father's domain?" "It may be I am wrong," said the Little Sage, "and if I am not, remember that devotion brings together dividing ways and that high hearts win to the end of every journey." He bade them goodby then, and turned back to his hut that was thatched with the great wing of a bird.

They rode across the Meadow of Brightness and Fedelma's blue falcon sailed above them. "Yonder is a field of white flowers," said she, "and while we are crossing it you must tell me a story."

"I know by heart," said the King's Son, "only the stories that Maravaun, my father's Councillor, has put into the book he is composing—the book that is called 'The Breastplate of Instruction.'"

"Then," said Fedelma, "tell me a story from 'The Breastplate of Instruction,' while we are crossing this field of white flowers."

"I will tell you the first story that is in it," said the King's Son.

Then while they were crossing the field of white flowers the King's Son told Fedelma the story of

THE ASS AND THE SEAL

X

A SEAL that had spent a curious forenoon paddling around the island of Ilaun-Beg drew itself up on a rock the better to carry on its investigations. It was now within five yards of the actual island. On the little beach there were three curraghs in which the island-men went over the sea; they were turned bottom up and heavy stones were placed upon them to prevent their being carried away by the high winds. The seal noted them as he rested upon the flat rock. He noted too a little ass that was standing beyond the curraghs, sheltering himself where the cliffs hollowed in.

Now this ass was as curious as the seal, and when he saw the smooth creature that was moving its head about with such intelligence he came down to the water's edge. Two of his legs were spancelled with a piece of straw rope, but being used to such impediment he came over without any awkwardness. He looked inquiringly at the seal.

The gray-headed crow of the cliff lighted on a spar of rock and made herself an interpreter between the two.

"Shaggy beast of the Island," said the seal, "friend and follower of men, tell me about their fabulous existence."

"Do you mean the hay-getters?" said the ass.

"You know well whom he means," said the gray-headed crow viciously. "Answer him now."

"You gravell me entirely when you ask about men," said the ass. "I don't know much about them. They live to themselves and I live to myself. Their houses are full of smoke and it blinds my eyes to go in. There used to be green fields here and high grass that became hay, but there's nothing like that now. I think men have given up eating what grows out of the ground. I see nothing, I smell nothing, but fish, fish, fish."

The gray-headed crow had a vicious eye fixed on the ass all the time he was speaking. "You're saying all that," said she, "because they let the little horse stay all night in the house and beat you out of it."

"My friend," said the seal, "it is evident that men deceive you by appearances. I know men. I have followed their boats and have listened to the wonderful sounds they make with their voices and with instruments. Do they not draw fish out of the depths by enchantments? Do they not build their habitations with music? Do they not draw the moon out of the sea and set it for a light in their houses? And is it not known that the fairest daughters of the sea have loved men?"

"When I'm awake long o' moonlit nights I feel like that myself," said the ass. Then the recollections of these long, frosty nights made him yawn. Then he brayed.

"What it is to live near men," said the seal in admiration. "What wonderful sounds!"

"I'd cross the water and rub noses with you," said the ass, "only I'm afraid of crocodiles."

"Crocodiles?" said the gray-headed crow.

"Yes," said the ass. "It's because I'm of a very old family, you know. They were Egyptians. My people never liked to cross water in their own country. There were crocodiles there."

"I don't want to waste any more time listening to nonsense," said the gray-headed crow. She flew to the ass's back and plucked out some of the felt. "I'll take this for my own habitation," she said, and flew back to the cliff.

The ass would have kicked up his heels only two of his legs were fastened with the straw rope. He turned away, and without a word of farewell to the seal went scrambling up the bank of the island.

The seal stayed for a while moving his head about intelligently. Then he slipped into the water and paddled off. "One feels their lives in music," he said; "great tones vibrate round the island where men live. It is very wonderful."

"That," said the King's Son, "is the first story in 'The Breastplate of Instruction,'—'The Ass and the Seal.' And now you must tell me a story while we are crossing the field of blue flowers."

"Then it will be a very little story," said Fedelma. They crossed a little field of blue flowers, and Fedelma told

THE SENDING OF THE CRYSTAL EGG

XI

THE Kings of Murias heard that King Atlas had to bear
The world upon his back, so they sent him then and
there
The Crystal Egg that would be the Swan of Endless Tales
That his burthen for a while might lie on his shoulder-
scales
Fair-balanced while he heard the Tales the Swan poured
forth—
North-world Tales for the while he watched the Star of
the North;
And East-world Tales he would hear in the morning swart
and cool,
When the Lions Nimrod had spared came up from the
drinking pool;

West-world Tales for the King when he turned him with
the sun;
Then whispers of magic Tales from Africa, his own.

But the Kings of Murias made the Crane their messenger—
The fitful Crane whose thoughts are always frightening
her:
She slipped from Islet to Isle, she sloped from Foreland to
Coast;
She passed through cracks in the mountains and came over
trees like a ghost;
And then fled back in dismay when she saw on the hollow
plains
The final battle between the Pigmies and the Cranes.

Where is the Crystal Egg that was sent King Atlas then?
Hatched it will be one day and the Tales will be told to
men:
That is if it be not laid in some King's old Treasury:
That is if the fitful Crane did not lose it threading the Sea!

They were not long going through the little field of
blue flowers, and when they went through it they came
to another field of white flowers. Fedelma asked the
King's Son to tell her another story, and thereupon he
told her the second story in "The Breastplate of Instruction."

THE STORY OF THE YOUNG CUCKOO

XII

THE young cuckoo made desperate attempts to get himself through the narrow opening in the hollow tree. He screamed when he failed to get through.

His foster parents had remained so long beside him that they were wasted and sad while the other birds, their broods reared, were vigorous and joyful. They heard the one that had been reared in their nest, the young cuckoo, scream, but this time they did not fly toward him. The young cuckoo screamed again, but there was something in that scream that reminded the foster parents of hawks. They flew away. They were miserable in their flight, these birds, for they knew they were committing a treason.

They had built their nest in a hollow tree that had a little opening. A cuckoo laid her egg on the ground and, carrying it in her beak, had placed it in the nest. Their own young had been pushed out. They had worn themselves to get provision for the terrible and fascinating creature who had remained in their nest.

When the time came for him to make his flight he could not get his body through the little opening. Yesterday he had begun to try. The two foster parents flew to him again and again with food. But now their own nesting place had become strange to them. They would never go near it again. The young cuckoo was forsaken.

A woodpecker ran round the tree. He looked into the hollow and saw the big bird crumpled up.

"Hello," said the woodpecker. "How did you get here?"

"Born here," said the young cuckoo sulkily.

"Oh, were you?" said the woodpecker and he ran round the tree again.

When he came back to the opening the young cuckoo was standing up with his mouth open.

"Feed me," said he.

"I've to rush round frightfully to get something for myself," said the woodpecker.

"At least, someone ought to bring me food," said the young cuckoo.

"How is that?" said the woodpecker.

"Well, oughtn't they to?" said the young cuckoo.

"I wouldn't say so," said the woodpecker, "you have

the use of your wits, haven't you?" He ran round the trunk of the tree again and devoured a lean grub. The young cuckoo struggled at the opening and screamed again.

"Don't be drawing too much attention to yourself," advised the woodpecker when he came to the opening again. "They might take you for a young hawk, you know."

"Who might?" said the cuckoo.

"The neighbors. They would pull a young hawk to pieces."

"What am I to do?" said the young cuckoo.

"What's in your nature to do?"

"My nature?" said the young cuckoo. "It's my nature to swing myself on branches high up in a tree. It's my nature to spread out my wings and fly over pleasant places. It is my nature to be alone. But not alone as here. Alone with the sound of my own voice." Suddenly he cried, "Cuckoo, cuckoo, cuckoo!"

"I know you now," said the woodpecker. "There's going to be a storm," he said; "trust a woodpecker to know that."

The young cuckoo strove toward the big sky again, and he screamed so viciously that a rat that had just come out of the ditch fastened his eyes on him. That creature looked bad to the young cuckoo. Rain plopped on the leaves. Thunder crashed. A bolt struck the tree, and the part above the opening was torn away.

The young cuckoo flung himself out on the grass and

went awkwardly amongst the blue bells. "What a world," said he. "All this wet and fire and noise to get me out of the nest. What a world!" The young cuckoo was free, and these were the first words he said when he went into the world.

That was the last story the King's Son told from Maravaun's book, "The Breastplate of Instruction." They had another little field of blue flowers to cross, and as they went across it Fedelma told the King's Son

THE STORY OF THE CLOUD WOMAN

XIII

THE Cloud-woman, Mor, was the daughter
  of Griann, the Sun,—well, and she
Made a marriage to equal that grandeur,
For her goodman was Lir, the Sea.

The Cloud-woman, Mor, she had seven
Strong sons, and the storybooks say
Their inches grew in the nighttime,
And grew over again in the day.

The Cloud-woman, Mor,—as they grew in
Their bone, she grew in her pride,
Till her haughtiness turned away, men say,
Her goodman Lir from her side;

Then she lived in Mor's House and she watched
With pride her sons and her crop,
Till one day the wish in her grew
To view from the mountain top
All, all that she owned, so she
Traveled without any stop.

And what did she see? A thousand
Fields and her own fields small, small!
"What a fine and wide place is Eirinn," said she,
"I am Mor, but not great after all."

Then a herdsman came, and he told her
That her sons had stolen away:
They had left the calves in the hollow,
With the goose flock they would not stay.

They had seen three ships on the sea
And nothing would do them but go:
Mor wept and wept when she heard it,
And her tears made runnels below.

Then her shining splendor departed:
She went, and she left no trace,
And the Cloud-woman, Mor, was never
Beheld again in that place.

The proud woman, Mor, who was daughter
Of Griann, the Sun, and who made
A marriage to equal that grandeur,
Passed away as a shade.

XIV

A ND that was the last story that Fedelma told, for they had crossed the Meadows of Brightness and had come to a nameless place—a stretch of broken ground where there were black rocks and dead grass and bare roots of trees with here and there a hawthorne tree in blossom. "I fear this place. We must not halt here," Fedelma said.

And then a flock of ravens came from the rocks, and flying straight at them attacked Fedelma and the King of Ireland's Son. The King's Son sprang from the steed and taking his sword in his hand he fought the ravens until he drove them away. They rode on again. But now the ravens flew back and attacked them again and the King of Ireland's Son fought them until his hands were wearied. He mounted the steed again, and they rode swiftly on. And the ravens came the third time and attacked them more fiercely than before. The King's Son fought them until he had killed all but three and until he was covered with their blood and feathers.

The three that had escaped flew away. "Oh, mount the Slight Red Steed and let us ride fast," said Fedelma to the King's Son.

"I am filled with weariness," he said. "Bid the steed stay by the rock, lay my sword at my side, and let me sleep with my head on your lap."

"I fear for us both if you slumber here," said Fedelma.

"I must sleep, and I pray that you let me lay my head on your lap."

"I know not what would awaken you if you slumber here."

"I will awaken," said the King's Son, "but now I must sleep, and I would slumber with my head on your lap."

She got down from the Slight Red Steed and she bade it stay by a rock; she put his sword by the place he would sleep and she took his head upon her lap. The King's Son slept.

As she watched over him a great fear grew in Fedelma. Every hour she would say to him, "Are you near waking, my dear, my dear?" But no flush of waking appeared on the face of the King of Ireland's Son.

Then she saw a man coming across the nameless place, across the broken ground, with its dead grass and black rocks and with its roots and stumps of trees. The man who came near them was taller than any man she had seen before—he was tall as a tree. Fedelma knew him from what she had heard told about him—she knew him to be the King of the Land of Mist.

The King of the Land of Mist came straight to them. He stood before Fedelma and he said, "I seek Fedelma, the daughter of the Enchanter of the Black Back-Lands and the fairest woman within the seas of Eirinn."

"Then go to her father's house and seek Fedelma there," said she to him.

"I have sought her there," said the King of the Land

of Mist, "but she left her father's house to go with the King of Ireland's Son."

"Then seek her in the Castle of the King of Ireland," said Fedelma.

"That I will not. Fedelma is here, and Fedelma will come with me," said the King of the Land of Mist.

"I will not leave him with whom I am plighted," said Fedelma.

Then the King of the Land of Mist took up the King of Ireland's Son. High he held him—higher than a tree grows. "I will dash him down on the rocks and break the life within him," said he.

"Do not so," said Fedelma. "Tell me. If I go with you what would win me back?"

"Nothing but the sword whose stroke would slay me —the Sword of Light," said the King of the Land of Mist. He held up the King of Ireland's Son again, and again he was about to dash him against the rocks. The blue falcon that was overhead flew down and settled on the rock behind her. Fedelma knew that what she and the King of the Land of Mist would say now would be carried some place and told to someone. "Leave my love, the King's Son, to his rest," she said.

"If I do not break the life in him will you come with me, Fedelma?"

"I will go with you if you tell again what will win me back from you."

"The Sword of Light whose stroke will slay me."

"I will go with you if you swear by all your vows and

promises not to make me your wife nor your sweetheart for a year and a day."

"I swear by all my vows and promises not to make you my wife nor my sweetheart for a year and a day."

"I will go with you if you let it be that I fall into a slumber that will last for a year and a day."

"I will let that be, fairest maid within the seas of Eirinn."

"I will go with you if you will tell me what will take me out of that slumber."

"If one cuts a tress of your hair with a stroke of the Sword of Light it will take you out of that slumber."

The blue falcon that was behind heard what the King of the Land of Mist said. She rose up and remained overhead with her wings outspread. Fedelma took the ring off her own finger and put it on the finger of the King of Ireland's Son, and she wrote upon the ground in Ogham letters, "The King of the Land of Mist."

"If it be not you who wakens me, love," she said, "may it be that I never waken."

"Come, daughter of the Enchanter," said the King of the Land of Mist.

"Pluck the branch of hawthorne and give it to me that I may fall into my slumber here," said Fedelma.

The King of the Land of Mist plucked a flowering branch of hawthorne and gave it to her. She held the flowers against her face and fell into slumber. For a while she and the King of Ireland's Son were side by side in sleep.

Then the King of the Land of Mist took Fedelma in his arms and strode along that nameless place, over the broken ground with its dead grass and its black rocks and its stumps and roots of trees and the three ravens that had escaped the sword of the King of Ireland's Son followed where he went.

XV

Long, long after Fedelma had been taken by the King of the Land of Mist the King of Ireland's Son came out of his slumber. He saw around him that nameless place with its black rocks and bare root of trees. He remembered he had come to it with Fedelma. He sprang up and looked for her, but no one was near him. "Fedelma, Fedelma!" He searched and he called, but it was as if no one had even been with him. He found his sword; he searched for his steed, but the Slight Red Steed was gone too.

He thought that the Enchanter of the Black Back-Lands had followed them and had taken Fedelma from him. He turned to go toward the Enchanter's country and then he found what Fedelma had written upon the ground in Ogham letters—

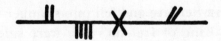

"The King of the Land of Mist"

He did not know what direction to take to get to the dominion of the King of the Land of Mist. He crossed the broken ground and he found no trace of Fedelma nor of him who had taken her. He found himself close to the Wood of Shadows. He went through it. As he went on he saw scores and scores of shadows. Nothing else was in the wood—no bird, no squirrel, no cricket. The shadows had the whole wood to themselves. They ran swiftly from tree to tree, and now and then one would stop at a tree and wait. Often the King of Ireland's Son came close to a waiting shadow. One became like a small old man with a beard. The King's Son saw this shadow again and again. What were they, the shadows, he asked himself? Maybe they were wise creatures and could tell him what he wanted to know.

He thought he heard them whispering together. Then one little shadow with trailing legs went slowly from tree to tree. The King of Ireland's Son thought he would catch and hold a shadow and make it tell him where he should go to find the dominion of the King of the Land of Mist.

He went after one shadow and another and waited beside a tree for one to come. Often he thought he saw the small old man with the beard and the little creature with trailing legs. And then he began to see other shadows—men with the heads of rooks and men with queer heavy swords upon their shoulders. He followed them on and on through the wood and he heard their whispering becoming louder and louder, and then he thought that as he went on the shadows, instead of slipping before him, began to turn back and go past and surround him. Then he heard a voice just under the ground at his feet say, "Shout—shout out your own name, Son of King Connal!" Then the King's Son shouted out his own name and the whispers ceased in the wood and the shadows went backward and forward no more.

He went on and came to a stream within the wood and he went against its flow all night as well as all day, hoping to meet some living thing that would tell him how he might come to the dominion of the King of the Land of Mist. In the forenoon of another day he came to where the wood grew thin and then he went past the last trees.

He saw a horse grazing: he ran up to it and found that it was the Slight Red Steed that had carried Fedelma and himself from the house of the Enchanter. Then as he laid hold of the steed a hound ran up to him and a hawk flew down and he saw that they were the hawk and the hound that used to be with him when he rode abroad from his father's Castle.

He mounted and seeing his hound at his heel and his hawk circling above he felt a longing to go back to his father's Castle which he knew to be near and where he might find out where the King of the Land of Mist had his dominion.

So the King of Ireland's Son rode back to his father's Castle—

>His hound at his heel,
>His hawk on his wrist.

WHEN THE KING
OF THE CATS CAME TO
KING CONNAL'S DOMINION

I

THE King of Ireland's Son was home again, but as he kept asking about a King and a Kingdom no one had ever heard of, people thought he had lost his wits in his search for the Enchanter of the Black Back-Lands. He rode abroad every day to ask strangers if they knew where the King of the Land of Mist had his dominion and he came back to his father's every night in the hope that one would be at the Castle who could tell him where the place that he sought was. Maravaun wanted to relate to him fables from "The Breastplate of Instruction" but the King's Son did not hear a word that Maravaun said. After a while he listened to the things that Art, the King's Steward, related to him, for it was Art who had shown the King's Son the leaden ring that was on his finger. He took it off, remembering the betrothal ring that the Little Sage had made, and then he saw that it was not his, but Fedelma's ring that he wore. Then he felt as if Fedelma had sent a message to him, and he was less wild in his thoughts.

Afterwards, in the evenings, when he came back

from his ridings, he would cross the meadows with Art, the King's Steward, or would stand with him while the herdsmen drove the cattle into the byres. Then he would listen to what Art related to him. And one evening he heard Art say, "The most remarkable event that happened was the coming into this land of the King of the Cats."

"I will listen to what you tell me about it," said the King's Son.

"Then," said Art, the King's Steward, "to your father's Son in all truth be it told"—

The King of the Cats stood up. He was a grand creature. His body was brown and striped across as if one had burned on wood with a hot poker. Like all the race of the Royal Cats of the Isle of Man he was without a tail. But he had extraordinarily fine whiskers. They went each side of his face to the length of a dinner dish. He had such eyes that when he turned one of them upward the bird that was flying across dropped from the sky. And when he turned the other one down he could make a hole in the floor.

He lived in the Isle of Man. Once he had been King of the Cats of Ireland and Britain, of Norway and Denmark, and the whole Northern and Western World. But after the Norsemen won in the wars the Cats of Norway and Britain swore by Thor and Odin that they would give him no more allegiance. So for a hundred years and a day he had got allegiance only from the Cats of the Western World; that is, from Ireland and the Islands beyond.

The tribute he received was still worth having. In May he was sent a boatful of herring. In August he was let have two boatfuls of mackerel. In November he was given five barrels of preserved mice. At other seasons he had for his tribute one out of every hundred birds that flew across the Island on their way to Ireland—tomtits, pee-wits, linnets, siskins, starlings, martins, wrens, and tender young barn owls. He was also sent the following as marks of allegiance and respect: a salmon, to show his dominion over the rivers; the skin of a marten to show his dominion in the woods; a live cricket to show his dominion in the houses of men; the horn of a cow, to show his right to a portion of the milk produced in the Western World.

But the tribute from the Western World became smaller and smaller. One year the boat did not come with the herring. Mackerel was sent to him afterwards but he knew it was sent to him because so much was being taken out of the sea that the farmermen were plowing their mackerel catches into the land to make their crops grow. Then a year came when he got neither the salmon nor the marten skin, neither the live cricket nor the cow's horn. Then he got righteously and royally indignant. He stood up on his four paws on the floor of his palace, and declared to his wife that he himself was going to Ireland to know what prevented the sending of his lawful tribute to him. He called for his Prime Minister then and said, "Prepare for Us our Speech from the Throne."

The Prime Minister went to the Parliament House and wrote down "Oyez, Oyez, Oyez!" But he could not remember any more of the ancient language in which the speeches from the Throne were always written. He went home and hanged himself with a measure of tape and his wife buried the body under the hearthstone.

"Speech or no speech," said the King of the Cats, "I'm going to pay a royal visit to my subjects in Ireland."

He went to the top of the cliff and he made a spring. He landed on the deck of a ship that was bringing the King of Norway's daughter to be married to the King of Scotland's son. The ship nearly sank with the crash of his body on it. He ran up the sails and placed himself on the mast of the ship. There he gathered his feet together and made another spring. This time he landed on a boat that was bringing oak-timber to build a King's Palace in London. He stood where the timber was highest and made another spring. This time he landed on the Giant's Causeway that runs from Ireland out into the sea. He picked his steps from boulder to boulder, and then walked royally and resolutely on the ground of Ireland. A man was riding on horseback with a woman seated on the saddle behind him. The King of the Cats waited until they came up.

"My good man," said he very grandly, when you go

back to your house, tell the ash-covered cat in the corner that the King of the Cats has come to Ireland to see him."

His manner was so grand that the man took off his hat and the woman made a courtesy. Then the King of the Cats sprang into the branch of a tree of the forest and slept till it was past the midday heat.

I nearly forgot to tell you that as he slept on the branch his whiskers stood around his face the breadth of a dinner dish either way.

II

THE next day the King's Son rode abroad and where he went that day he saw no man nor woman nor living creature in the land around. But coming back he saw a falcon sailing in the air above. He rode on and the falcon sailed above, never rising high in the air, and never swooping down. The King's Son fitted an arrow to his bow and shot at the falcon. Immediately it rose in the air and flew swiftly away, but a feather from it fell before him. The King's Son picked the feather up. It was a blue feather. Then the King's Son thought of Fedelma's falcon—of the bird that flew above them when they rode across the Meadows of Brightness. It might be Fedelma's falcon, the one that he had shot at, and it might have come to show him the way to the Land of Mist. But the falcon was not to be seen now.

He did not go amongst the strangers in his father's

Castle that evening; but he stood with Art who was watching the herdsmen drive the cattle into the byres. And Art after a while said, "I will tell you more about the coming of the King of the Cats into King Connal's Dominion. And as before I say

"To your father's Son in all truth be it told"—

The King of the Cats waited on the branch of the tree until the moon was in the sky like a roast duck on a dish of gold, and still neither retainer, vassal nor subject came to do him service. He was vexed, I tell you, at the want of respect shown him.

This was the reason why none of his subjects came to him for such a long time: The man and woman he had spoken to went into their house and did not say a word about the King of Cats until they had eaten their supper. Then when the man had smoked his second pipe, he said to the woman:

"That was a wonderful thing that happened to us today. A cat to walk up to two Christians and say to them, 'Tell the ashy pet in your chimney corner at home that the King of the Cats has come to see him.'"

No sooner were the words said than the lean, gray, ash-covered cat that lay on the hearthstone sprang on the back of the man's chair.

"I will say this," said the man; "it's a bad time when two Christians like ourselves are stopped on their way back from the market and ordered—ordered, no less —to give a message to one's own cat lying on one's own hearthstone."

"By my fur and claws, you're a long time coming to his message," said the cat on the back of the chair; "what was it, anyway?"

"The King of the Cats has come to Ireland to see you," said the man, very much surprised.

"It's a wonder you told it at all," said the cat, going to the door. "And where did you see His Majesty?"

"You shouldn't have spoken," said the man's wife.

"And how did I know a cat could understand?" said the man.

"When you have done talking amongst yourselves," said the cat, "would you tell me where you met His Majesty?"

"Nothing will I tell you," said the man, "until I hear your own name from you."

"My name," said the cat, "is Quick-to-Grab, and well you should know it."

"Not a word will we tell you," said the woman, "until we hear what the King of the Cats is doing in Ireland. Is he bringing wars and rebellions into the country?"

"Wars and rebellions—no, ma'am," said Quick-to-Grab, "but deliverance from oppression. Why are the cats of the country lean and lazy and covered with ashes? It is because the cat that goes outside the house in the sunlight, to hunt or to play, is made to suffer with the loss of an eye."

"And who makes them suffer with the loss of an eye?" said the woman.

"One whose reign is nearly over now," said Quick-to-Grab. "But tell me where you saw His Majesty?"

"No," said the man.

"No," said the woman, "for we don't like your impertinence. Back with you to the hearthstone, and watch the mouse hole for us."

Quick-to-Grab walked straight out of the door.

"May no prosperity come to this house," said he, "for denying me when I asked where the King of the Cats was pleased to speak to you."

But he put his ear to the door when he went outside and he heard the woman say—

"The horse will tell him that we saw the King of the Cats a mile this side of the Giant's Causeway."

(That was a mistake. The horse could not have told it at all, because horses never know the language that is spoken in houses—only cats know it fully and dogs know a little of it.)

Quick-to-Grab now knew where the King of the Cats might be found. He went creeping by hedges, loping across fields, bounding through woods, until he came under the branch in the forest where the King of the Cats rested, his whiskers standing round his face the breadth of a dinner-dish.

When he came under the branch Quick-to-Grab mewed a little in Egyptian, which is the ceremonial language of the Cats. The King of the Cats came to the end of the branch.

"Who are you, vassal?" said he in Phœnician.

"A humble retainer of my lord," said Quick-to-Grab in High-Pictish (this is a language very suitable to cats but it is only their historians who now use it).

They continued their conversation in Irish.

"What sign shall I show the others that will make them know you are the King of the Cats?" said Quick-to-Grab.

The King of the Cats chased up the tree and pulled down heavy branches. "There is a sign of my royal prowess," said he.

"It's a good sign," said Quick-to-Grab.

They were about to talk again when Quick-to-Grab put down his tail and ran up another tree greatly frightened.

"What ails you?" said the King of the Cats. "Can you not stay still while you are speaking to your lord and master?"

"Old-fellow Badger is coming this way," said Quick-to-Grab, "and when he puts his teeth in one he never lets go."

Without saying a word the King of the Cats jumped down from the tree. Old-fellow Badger was coming through the glade. When he saw the King of the Cats crouching there he stopped and bared his terrible teeth. The King of the Cats bent himself to spring. Then Old-fellow Badger turned round and went lumbering back.

"Oh, by my claws and fur," said Quick-to-Grab, "you are the real King of the Cats. Let me be your

Councillor. Let me advise your Majesty in the times that will be so difficult for your subjects and yourself. Know that the Cats of Ireland are impoverished and oppressed. They are under a terrible tyranny."

"Who oppresses my vassals, retainers, and subjects?" said the King of the Cats.

"The Eagle-Emperor. He has made a law that no cat may leave a man's house as long as the birds (he makes an exception in the case of owls) have any business abroad."

"I will tear him to pieces," said the King of the Cats. "How can I reach him?"

"No cat has thought of reaching him," said Quick-to-Grab, "they only think of keeping out of his way. Now let me advise your Majesty. None of our enemies must know that you have come into this country. You must appear as a common cat."

"What, me?" said the King of the Cats.

"Yes, your Majesty, for the sake of the deliverance of your subjects you will have to appear as a common cat."

"And be submissive and eat scraps?"

"That will be only in the daytime," said Quick-to-Grab, "in the nighttime you will have your court and your feasts."

"At least, let the place I stay in be no hovel," said the King of the Cats. "I shall refuse to go into a house where there are washing days—damp clothes before a fire and all that."

"I shall use my best diplomacy to safeguard your

comfort and dignity," said Quick-to-Grab, "please in-
vest me as your Prime Minister."

The King of the Cats invested Quick-to-Grab by
biting the fur round his neck. Then the King and his
Prime Minister parted. The King of the Cats took up
quarters for a day or two in a round tower. Quick-to-
Grab made a journey through the countryside. He went
into every house and whispered a word to every cat
that was there, and whether the cat was watching a
mouse hole, or chasing crickets, or playing with kittens,
when he or she heard that word they sat up and
considered.

III

EARLY, early, next day the King of Ireland's Son rode
out in search of the blue falcon, but although he
rode from the ring of day to the gathering of the dark
clouds he saw no sign of it on rock or tree or in the air.
Very wearily he rode back, and after his horse was
stabled he stood with Art in the meadows watching the
cattle being driven by. And Art, the King's Steward,
said: "The Coming of the King of the Cats into King
Connal's dominion is a story still to be told.

"To your father's Son in all truth be it told"—

Quick-to-Grab, in consultation with the Seven Elders
of the Cat-Kin decided that the Blacksmith's forge
would be a fit residence for the King of the Cats. It was

clean and commodious. But the best reason of all for his going there was this: people and beasts from all parts came into the forge and the King of the Cats might learn from their discussions where the Eagle-Emperor was and how he might be destroyed.

His Majesty found that the Forge was not a bad residence for a King living unbeknownst. It was dry and warm. He liked the look of the flames that mounted up with the blowing of the bellows. He used to sit on a heap of old saddles on the floor and watch the horses being shod or waiting to be shod. He listened to the talk of the men. The people in the Forge treated him respectfully and often referred to his size, his appearance and his fine manners.

Every night he went out to a feast that the cats had prepared for him. Quick-to-Grab always walked back to the Forge with him to give a Prime Minister's advice. He warned His Majesty not to let the human beings know that he understood and could converse in their language— (all cats know men's language, but men do not know that the cats know). He told them not to be too haughty (as a King might be inclined to be) to any creature in the Forge.

The King of the Cats took this advice. He used even to twitch his ears as a mark of respect to Mahon, the hound whose kennel was just outside the Forge, and to the hounds that Mahon had to visit him. He even made advances to the Cock who walked up and down outside.

This Cock made himself very annoying to the King

of the Cats. He used to strut up and down saying to himself over and over again, "I'm Cock-o'-the-Walk, I'm Cock-o'-the-Walk." Sometimes he would come into the Forge and say it to the horses. The King of the Cats wondered how the human beings could put up with a creature who was so stupid and so vain. He had a red comb that fell over one eye. He had purple feathers on his tail. He had great spurs on his heels. He used to put his head on one side and yawn when the King of the Cats appeared.

Cock-o'-the-Walk used to come into the Forge at night and sleep on the bellows. And when the King of the Cats came back from the feasts he used to waken up and say to himself, "I'm Cock-o'-the-Walk, I'm Cock-o'-the-Walk. The Cats are not a respectable people."

One noonday there were men in the Forge. They were talking to the Smith. Said one, "Could you tell us, Smith, where iron came from?"

The King of the Cats knew but he said nothing. Cock-o'-the-Walk came to the door and held his head as if he were listening.

"I can't tell where iron came from," said the Smith, "but if that Cock could talk he could tell you. The world knows that the Cock is the wisest and the most ancient of creatures."

"I'm Cock-o'-the-Walk," said the Cock to a rusty ass's shoe.

"Yes, the Cock is a wonderful creature," said the man who had asked the question.

"Not wonderful at all," said the King of the Cats, "and if you had asked me I could have told you where iron came from."

"And where did iron come from?" said the Smith.

"From the Mountains of the Moon," said the King of the Cats.

The men in the Forge put their hands on their knees and looked down at him. Mahon the hound came into the Forge with other hounds at his tail, and seeing the men looking at the King of the Cats, Mahon put his nose to him. Cock-o'-the-Walk flapped his wings insolently. The King of the Cats struck at the red hanging comb with his paw. The Cock flew up in the air. The King of the Cats sprang out of the window, and as he did, Mahon and the other hounds sprang after him—

IV

THE King of Ireland's Son rode toward the East the next day, and in the first hour's journey he saw the blue falcon sailing above. He followed where it went and the falcon never lifted nor stooped, but sailed steadily on, only now and again beating the air with its wings. Over benns and through glens and across moors the blue falcon flew and the King of Ireland's Son followed. Then his horse stumbled; he could not go any further, and he lost sight of the blue falcon.

Black night was falling down on the ground when he came back to the King's Castle. Art, the King's Steward, was waiting for him and he walked beside his limping horse. And Art said when they were a little way together, "The Coming of the King of the Cats is a story still to be told.

"To your father's Son in all truth be it told"—

By the magic powers they possessed it was made known to all the cats in the country that their King was being pursued by the hounds. Then on every hearthstone a cat howled. Cats sprang to the doors, overturning cradles upon children. They stood upon the thresholds and they all made the same curse—"That ye may break your backs, that ye may break your backs before ye catch the King of the Cats."

When he heard the howls of his vassals, retainers and subjects, the King of the Cats turned over on his back and clawed at the first hound that came after him. He stood up then. So firmly did he set himself on his four legs that those that dashed at him did not overthrow him. He humped up his body and lifted his forepaws. The hounds held back. A horn sounded and that gave them an excuse to get away from the claws and the teeth, the power and the animosity of the King of the Cats.

Then, even though it might cost each and every one of them the loss of an eye, the cats that had sight of him came running up. "We will go with you, my lord, we will help you, my lord," they cried all together.

"Go back to the hearthstones," said the King of the

Cats. "Go back and be civil and quiet again in the houses. You will hear of my deeds. I go to find the tracks of our enemy, the Eagle-Emperor."

When they heard that announcement the cats lamented, and the noise of their lamentation was so dreadful that horses broke their harnesses where they were yoked; men and women lost the color of their faces thinking some dreadful visitation was coming on the land; every bag of oats and rye turned five times to the right and five times to the left with the fright it got; dishes were broken, knives were hurled round, and the King's Castle was shaken to the bottom stone.

"It is not the time to seek the tracks of the Eagle-Emperor," said Quick-to-Grab. "Stay for a while longer in men's houses."

"Never," said the King of the Cats. "Never will I stay by the hearthstone and submit to be abused by cocks and hounds and men. I will range the world openly now and seek out the enemy of the Cat-Kind, the Eagle-Emperor."

Without once turning his back he went toward the wood that was filled with his enemies, the birds. The cats, when they saw their petitions were no use, went everyone back to the house where he or she stayed. Each one sat before a mouse hole and pretended to be watching. But though mice stirred all round them the cats of Ireland never turned a head that night.

It was the wren, the smallest of birds, that saw him and knew him for the King of the Cats. The wren flew through the wood to summon the Hawk-Clan. But it was toward sunset now and the hawks had taken up their stations at the edge of the wood to watch that they might pick up the farmers' chickens. They wouldn't turn an eye when the wren told them that a cat was in the wood during the time forbidden to cats to be outside the houses of men. "It is the King of the Cats," said the wren. None of the hawks lifted a wing. They were waiting for the chickens that would stray about the moment after sunset.

But if the wren couldn't rouse the Hawk-Clan she was able to rouse the other bird-tribes. "A cat, a cat, on your lives a cat," she called out as she flew through the wood. The rooks that were going home now rose above the trees, cawing threats. The blackbirds, thrushes, and jays screamed as they flew before the King of the Cats. The woodpeckers, hedge-sparrows, tom-tits, robins, and linnets chattered as they flew behind him. Sometimes the young rooks made a great show of attacking him. They flew down from the flock. "He is here, here, here," they cawed and flew up again. The rooks kept telling themselves and the other birds in the wood what they were going to do with the King of the Cats. But a single raven did more against him than the thousand rooks that made so much noise. This raven was in a hole in the tree. She struck the King of the Cats on the head with her beak as he went past.

The King of the Cats was annoyed by the uproar the birds were making and he was angered by the raven's stroke, but he did not want to enter into a battle with the birds. He was on his way to the house of the Hag of the Wood who was then known as the Hag of the Ashes. Now as this is the first time you have heard of the Hag of the Ashes, I'll have to tell you how the King of the Cats had heard of her and how he knew where her house was in the wood.

V

THE next day the King's Son put a bridle on the Slight Red Steed and rode toward the East again. He saw the blue falcon and he followed where it flew. Over benns, and through glens, and across mountains and moors the blue falcon went and the Slight Red Steed neither swerved nor stumbled but went as the bird flew. The falcon lighted on a pine tree that grew alone. The King's Son rode up and put his hands to the tree to climb and put his head against it, and as he did he heard speech from the tree. "The stroke of the Sword of Light will slay the King of the Land of Mist and the stroke of the Sword of Light that will cut a tress of her hair will awaken Fedelma." There was no more speech from the tree and the falcon rose from its branches and flew high up in the air. Then the King of Ireland's Son rode back toward his father's Castle.

He went to the meadow and stood with Art and listened to what Art had to tell him. And as before the King's Steward began—

"To your father's Son in all truth be it told"—

Quick-to-Grab had said to the King of the Cats, "If ever you need the counsel of a human being, go to no one else but the Hag of the Ashes who was once called the Hag of the Wood. In the very center of the wood four ash trees are drawn together at the tops, wattles are woven round these ash trees, and in the little house made in this way the Hag of the Ashes lives, with no one near her since her nine daughters went away, but her goat that's her only friend." The King of the Cats was now in the center of the wood. He saw four ash trees drawn together at the tops and he jumped to them.

Now the Hag of the Ashes had a bad neighbor. This was a crane that had built her nest across the roof of the little house. The nest prevented the smoke from coming out at the top and the house below was filled with it. The Hag could hardly keep alive on account of the smoke and she could neither take away the nest nor banish the bird.

The crane was there when the King of the Cats sprang on the roof. She was sitting with her two legs stretched out, and when the King of the Cats came down beside her she slipped away and sailed over the trees. "Time for me to be going," said the crane. And from that day to this she never came back to the house of the Hag of the Ashes.

"Oh, thanks to you, good creature," said the Hag of the Ashes, coming out of the house. "Tear down her nest now and let the smoke rise up through the roof."

The King of the Cats tore up the sticks and wool that the crane's nest was made of, and the smoke came up through the top of the house. "Oh, thanks to you, good creature, that has destroyed the cross crane's nest. Come down on my floor now and I'll do everything that will serve you."

The King of the Cats jumped down on the floor of the Hag's house and saw the Hag of the Ashes sitting in a corner. She was a little, little woman in a gray cloak. All over the floor there were ashes in heaps, for she used to light a fire in one corner and when it was burnt out light another beside the ashes of the first. The smoke had never gone through the hole in the roof since the crane had built her nest on the top of the house. Her face was yellow with the smoke and her eyes were half closed on account of it.

"Do you know who I am, Hag of the Ashes?" said the King of the Cats when he stood on the floor.

"You are a cat, honey," said the Hag of the Ashes.

"I am the King of the Cats."

"The King of the Cats you are indeed. And it was you who let the smoke out of the top of my little house by destroying the nest the cross crane had built on it."

"It was I who did that."

"Welcome to you then, King of the Cats. And what service can the Hag of the Ashes do for you in return?"

"I would go to where the Eagle-Emperor is. You must show me the way."

"By my cloak I will do that. The Eagle-Emperor lives on the top of the Hill of Horns."

"And how can I get to the top of the Hill of Horns?"

"I don't know how you can get there at all. All over the Hill is bare starvation. No four-footed thing can reach the top—no four-footed thing, I mean, but my goat that's tied to the hawthorn bush outside."

"I will ride on the back of your goat to the top of the Hill of Horns."

"No, no, good King of the Cats. I have only my goat for company and how could I bear to be parted from him?"

"Lend me your goat, and when I come back from the Hills of Horns I will plate his horns with gold and shoe his hooves with silver."

"No, no, good King of the Cats. How could I bear my goat to be away from me, and I having no other company?"

"If you do not let me ride on your goat to the top of the Hill of Horns I will leave a sign on your house that will bring the cross crane to build her nest on the top of it again."

"Then take my goat, King of the Cats, take my goat but let him come back to me soon."

"I will. Come with me now and bid him take me to the top of the Hill of Horns."

The King of the Cats marched out of the house and the Hag of the Ashes hobbled after him. The goat was lying under the hawthorn bush. He put his horns to the ground when they came up to him.

"Will you go to the Hill of Horns?" said the Hag of the Ashes.

"Indeed, that I will not do," said the goat.

"Oh, the soft tops of the hedges on the way to the Hill of Horns—sweet in the mouth of a goat they should be," said the Hag of the Ashes. "But my own poor goat wants to stay here and eat the tops of the burnt-up thistles."

"Why didn't you tell me of the hedges on the way to the Hill of Horns before?" said the goat, rising to his feet. "To the Hill of Horns I'll go."

"And will you let a cat ride on your back to the Hill of Horns?"

"Indeed, I will not do that."

"Then, my poor goat, I'll not untie the rope that's round your neck, for you can't go to the Hill of Horns without this cat riding on your back."

"Let him sit on my back then and hold my horns, and I'll take no notice of him."

The Hag of the Ashes untied the rope that was round his neck, the King of the Cats jumped up on the goat's back, and they started off on the path through the wood. "Oh, how I'll miss my goat, until he comes back to me with gold on his horns and silver on his hooves," the Hag of the Ashes cried after them.

VI

THE King of Ireland's Son did not leave the Castle the next day, but stayed to question those who came to it about the Sword of Light. And some had heard of the Sword of Light and some had not heard of it. In the afternoon he was in the chambers of the Castle and he watched his two foster brothers, Dermott and Downal, the sons of Caintigern, the Queen, playing chess. They played the game upon his board and with his figures. And when he went up to them and told them they had permission to use the board and the figures, they said, "We had forgotten that you owned these things." The King's Son saw that everything in the Castle was coming into the possession of his foster brothers.

He found another board with other chessmen and he played a game with the King's Steward. And Art said, "The coming of the King of the Cats into King Connal's Dominion is a story still to be told.

"To your father's Son in all truth be it told"—

What should a goat do but ramble down laneways, wander across fields, stray along hedges and stay to rest under shady trees? All this the Hag's goat did. But at last he brought the King of the Cats to the foot of the Hill of Horns.

And what was the Hill of Horns like, asks my kind foster child. It was hills of stones on the top of a hill of stones. Only a goat could foot it from pebble to stone, from stone to boulder, from boulder to crag, and from crag to mountain-shoulder. It was well and not ill what the Hag's goat did. But then thunder sounded; lightning struck fire out of the stones, the wind mixed itself with the rain and the tempest pelted cat and goat. The goat

stood on a mountain-shoulder. The wind rushed up from
the bottom and carried the companions to the top of the
Hill of Horns. Down sprang the cat. But the goat stood
on his hind legs to butt back at the wind. The wind
caught him between the beard and the underquarters
and swept him from the top and down the other side
of the hill (and what happened to the Hag's goat after
this I never heard). The King of the Cats put his claws
into the crevices of a standing stone and held to it with
great tenacity. And then, when the wind abated and he
looked across his shoulder, he found that he was standing beside the nest of the Eagle-Emperor.

It was a hollow edged with rocks, and round that
hollow were scattered the horns of the deer and goats
that the Eagle-Emperor had carried off. And in the hollow there was a calf and a hare and a salmon. The King
of the Cats sprang into the Eagle-Emperor's nest. First
he ate the salmon. Then he stretched himself between
the hare and the calf and waited for the Eagle-Emperor.

At last he appeared. Down he came to the nest making
circles in the air. He lighted on the rocky rim. The King
of the Cats rose with body bent for the spring, and if
the Eagle-Emperor was not astonished at his appearance
it was because an Eagle can never be astonished.

A brave man would be glad if he could have seen the
Eagle-Emperor as he crouched there on the rock rim of
his nest. He spread down his wings till they were great
strong shields. He bent down his outspread tail. He bent
down his neck so that his eyes might look into the crea-

ture that faced him. And his cruel, curved, heavy beak was ready for the stroke.

But the King of the Cats sprang into the air. The Eagle lifted himself up but the Cat came down on his broad back. The Eagle-Emperor screamed his war-scream and flew off the hill. He struck at the King of the Cats with the backs of his broad wings. Then he plunged down. On the stones below he would tear his enemy with beak and claws.

It was the Cat that reached the ground. As the Eagle went to strike at him he sprang again and tore the Eagle's breast. Then the Eagle-Emperor caught the King of the Cats in his claws and flew up again, screaming his battle-scream. Drops of blood from both fell on the ground. The Eagle had not a conquerer's grip on his enemy and the King of the Cats was able to tear at him.

It happened that Curoi, King of the Munster Fairies, was marching at the head of his troop to play a game of hurling with the Fianna of Ireland, captained by Fergus, and for the hand of Ainé, the daughter of Mananaun, the Lord of the Sea. Just when the ball was about to be thrown in the air the Eagle-Emperor and the King of the Cats were seen mixed together in their struggle. One troop took the side of the Eagle and the other took the side of the Cat. The men of the country came up and took sides too. Then the men began to fight amongst themselves and some were left dead on the ground. And this went on until there were hosts of the men of Ireland fighting each other on account of the Eagle-Emperor and the King of the Cats. The King of the Fairies and the

Chief of the Fianna marched their men away to a hill top where they might watch the battle in the air and the battles on the ground. "If this should go on," said Curoi, "our troops will join in and men and Fairies will be slaughtered. We must end the combat in the air." Saying this he took up the hurling-ball and flung it at the Cat and Eagle. Both came down on the ground. The Cat was about to spring, the Eagle was about to pounce, when Curoi darted between them and struck both with his spear. Eagle and Cat became figures of stone. And there they are now, a Stone Eagle with his wings outspread and a Stone Cat with his teeth bared and his paws raised. And the Eagle-Emperor and the King of Cats will remain like that until Curoi strikes them again with his fairy spear.

When the Cat and the Eagle were turned into stone the men of the country wondered for a while and then they went away. And the Fairies of Munster and the Fianna of Ireland played the hurling match for the hand of Ainé the daughter of Mananaun who is Lord of the Sea, and what the result of that hurling match was is told in another book.

And that ends my history of the coming into Ireland of the King of the Cats.

The King of Ireland's Son left Art and went into an unused room in the Castle to search for a little bell that he might put upon the Slight Red Steed. He found the little bell, but it fell out of his hand and slipped through a crack in the floor. He went and looked through the crack. He saw below a room and in it was Caintigern, the Queen, and beside her were two women in the cloaks of enchantresses. And when he looked again he knew the two of them—they were Aefa and Gilveen, the daughters of the Enchanter of the Black Back-Lands and Fedelma's sisters. "And will my two sons come to rule over their father's dominion?" he heard Caintigern ask.

"The Prince who gains the Sword of Light will rule over his father's dominion," Aefa said.

"Then one of my sons must get the Sword of Light," Caintigern said. "Tell me where they must go to get knowledge of where it is."

"Only the Gobaun Saor knows where the Sword of Light is," said Aefa.

"The Gobaun Saor! Can he be seen by men?" said Caintigern.

"He can be seen," said Aefa. "And there is one—the Little Sage of the Mountain—who can tell what road to go to find the Gobaun Saor."

"Then," said Caintigern, "my two sons, Dermott and Downal, will ride out tomorrow to find the Little Sage of the Mountain, and the Gobaun Saor, so that one of them may find the Sword of Light and come to rule over his father's dominion."

When the King of Ireland's Son heard that, he went to the stable where the Slight Red Steed was, and put the bridle upon him and rode toward the Hill of Horns, on one side of which was the house thatched with the one great wing of a bird, where the Little Sage of the Mountain lived.

THE SWORD OF LIGHT AND THE UNIQUE TALE, WITH AS MUCH OF THE ADVENTURES OF GILLY OF THE GOATSKIN AS IS GIVEN IN "THE CRANESKIN BOOK"

I

HE came to the house that was thatched with the one great wing of a bird, and, as before, the Little Sage of the Mountain asked him to do a day's work. The King's Son reaped the corn for the Little Sage, and as he was reaping it his two foster brothers, Dermott and Downal, rode by on their fine horses. They did not know who the young fellow was who was reaping in the field and they shouted for the Little Sage of the Mountain to come out of the house and speak to them. "We want to know where to find the Gobaun Saor who is to give us the Sword of Light," said Dermott.

"Come in," said the Sage, "and help me with my day's work, and I'll search in my book for some direction."

"We can't do such an unprincely thing as take service with you," said Downal. "Tell us now where we must go to find the Gobaun Saor."

"I think you have made a mistake," said the Little Sage. "I'm an ignorant man, and I can't answer such a question without study."

"Ride on, brother," said Downal, "he can tell us nothing."

Dermott and Downal rode off on their fine horses, the silver bells on their bridles ringing.

That night, when he had eaten his supper, the Little Sage told the King's Son where to go. It is forbidden to tell where the King of Ireland's Son found the Builder and Shaper for the Gods. In a certain place he came to where the Gobaun Saor had set up his forge and planted his anvil, and he saw the Gobaun Saor beating on a shape of iron.

"You want to find the Sword of Light," said the Gobaun, his eyes as straight as the line of a sword blade, "but show me first your will, your mind, and your purpose."

"How can I do that?" said the King of Ireland's Son.

"Guard my anvil for a few nights," said the Gobaun Saor. "A Fua comes out of the river sometimes and tries to carry it off."

The Gobaun Saor had to make a journey to look at trees that were growing in the forest, and the King's Son guarded his anvil. And at night a Fua came out of the river and flung great stones, striving to drive him away from the anvil. He ran down to the river bank to drive it away, but the creature caught him in its long arms and tried to drown him in the deep water. The King of Ireland's Son was near his death, but he broke away from the Fua, and when the creature caught him again, he dragged it up the bank and held it against a tree. "I will give you the mastery of all arts because you have mastered me," said the Fua. "I do not want the mastery of

The creature caught him in its long arms.

arts, but maybe you can tell me where to find the Sword of Light." "You want to know that—do you?" said the Fua, and then it twisted from him and went into the river.

The Fua came the next night and flung stones as before, and the King's Son wrestled with it in the very middle of the river, and held him so that he could not get to the other bank. "I will give you heaps of wealth because you have mastered me," said the creature with the big eyes and the long arms. "Not wealth, but the knowledge of where to come on the Sword of Light is what I want from you," said the King of Ireland's Son. But the Fua twisted from him and ran away again.

The next night the Fua came again, and the King's Son wrestled with him in the middle of the river and followed him up the other bank, and held him against a tree. "I will give you the craft that will make you the greatest of Kings, because you have mastered me." "Not craft, but knowledge of where the Sword of Light is, I want from you," said the King's Son. "Only one of the People of Light can tell you that," said the Fua. It became a small, empty sort of creature and lay on the ground like a shadow.

The Gobaun Saor came back to his forge and his anvil. "You have guarded my anvil for me," he said, "and I will tell you where to go for the Sword of Light. It is in the Palace of the Ancient Ones under the Lake. You have an enchanted steed that can go to that Lake. I shall turn his head, and he shall go straight to it. When you

come to the edge of the Lake pull the branches of the
Fountain Tree and give the Slight Red Steed the leaves
to eat. Mount now and go."

The King of Ireland's Son mounted the Slight Red
Steed and went traveling again.

II

FROM all its branches, high and low, water was falling
in little streams. This was the Fountain Tree indeed.
He did not dismount, the King of Ireland's Son, but
pulled the branches and he gave them to the Slight Red
Steed to eat.

He ate no more than three mouthfuls. Then he
stamped on the ground with his hooves, lifted his head
high and neighed three times. With that he plunged
into the water of the Lake and swam and swam as if he
had the strength of a dragon. He swam while there was
light on the water and he swam while there was night
on the water, and when the sun of the next day was a
hand's breadth above the lake he came to the Black Island.

All on that Island was black and burnt, and there were
black ashes up to the horse's knees. And no sooner had
the Slight Red Steed put his hooves on the Island than
he galloped straight to the middle of it. He galloped
through an opening in the black rock and went through
a hundred passages, each going lower than the other, and
at last he came into the wide space of a hall.

The hall was lighted. When the King's Son looked

to see where the light came from he saw a sword hanging from the roof. And the brightness of the Sword was such that the hall was well lighted. The King of Ireland's Son galloped the Slight Red Steed forward and made it rear up. His hand grasped the hilt of the Sword. As he pulled it down the Sword screeched in his hand.

He flashed it about and saw what other things were in the Cave. He saw one woman, and two women, and three women. He came to them and he saw they were sleeping. And as he flashed the Sword about he saw other women sleeping too. There were twelve women in the Cave where the Sword of Light had been hanging and the women were sleeping.

And in the hands of each of the sleeping women was a great gemmed cup. The spirit of the King's Son had grown haughty since he felt the Sword in his hands. "You have the sword, why should you not have the cup?" something within him said. He took a cup from the hands of one of the sleeping women and drank the bubbling water that is held. His spirit grew more haughty with that draught. From the hands of each of the twelve sleeping women he took the cup and he drank the draught of bubbling water that it held. And when he had drunk the twelve draughts of bubbling water he felt that with the Sword of Light in his hands he could cut his way through the earth.

He mounted the Slight Red Steed and rode it through the Cave and swam it across the Lake with No Name. He held the Sword of Light across his saddle. The Steed went as the current drew him, for it was long since he had eaten the leaves of the Fountain Tree, and the spirit that had made him vigorous coming was feeble now. The current brought them to the shore below where the Fountain Tree grew.

And there on the shore he saw a bunch of little men, little women and littler children, all with smoke-colored skins, all with but one eye in their heads, all crying and screaming at each other like seabirds, and all sitting round a fire of dried water weeds, cooking and eating eels and crab-apples.

The King of Ireland's Son put his hands on the bridle-rein and drew the Slight Red Steed out of the water. The women with one right eye and the men with one left eye, and the children in their bare smoky skins screamed at him, "What do you want, what do you want, man with the horse?"

"Feed and water my steed for me," said the King of Ireland's Son.

"We are the Swallow People, and no one commands us to do things," said an old fellow with a beard like knots of ropes.

"Feed my steed with red wheat and water it with pure spring water," said the King's Son fiercely. "I am the King of Ireland's Son and the Sword of Light is in my hands, and what I command must be done."

"We are the Swallow People and we are accounted a harmless people," said the old fellow.

"Why are ye harmless?" said the King's Son, and he flourished the sword at them.

"Come into our cave, King's Son," said the old fellow, "we will give you refreshment there, and the children will attend to your steed."

He went into the cave with certain of the Swallow People. They were all unmannerly. They kept screaming and crying to each other; they pulled at the clothes of the King's Son and pinched him. One of them bit his hands. When they came into the cave they all sat down on black stones. One pulled in a black ass loaded with nets. They took the nets off its back, and before the King's Son knew that anything was about to happen they threw the nets around him. The meshes of the nets were sticky. He felt himself caught. He ran at the Swallow People and fell over a stone. They then drew more nets around his legs.

The old fellow whom he had commanded took up the Sword of Light. Then the Swallow People pulled up the ass that had carried the nets and rubbed its hard hoof on the Sword. The King's Son did not know what happened to it. Then he heard them cry, "The brightness is gone off the thing now." They left the Sword on a black rock, and now no light came from it. Then all the Swallow People scrambled out of the cave.

They came back eating eels and crabapples out of their hands. They paid no attention to the King of Ireland's Son, but climbed into a cave above where he was lying.

He broke the nets that were round him. He found the Sword on the black stones, with the brightness all gone from it because of the rubbing with the ass's hoof. He climbed up the wall of the other cave to punish the Swallow People. They saw him before he could see them in the darkness, and they all went into holes and hid themselves as if they were rats and mice.

With the blackened sword in his hands the King of Ireland's Son went out of the Cave, and the horse he had left behind, the Slight Red Steed, was not to be found.

III

WITHOUT a steed and with a blackened sword the King of Ireland's Son came to where the Gobaun Saor had set up his forge and planted his anvil. No water nor sand would clean the Sword, but he left it down before the Gobaun Saor, hoping that he would show him a way to clean it. "The Sword must be bright that will kill the King of the Land of Mist and cut the tress that will awaken the Enchanter's daughter," said the Gobaun Saor. "You have let the Sword be blackened. Carry the blackened Sword with you now."

"Brighten it for me and I will serve you," said the King of Ireland's Son.

"It is not easy for me to brighten the Sword now," said the Gobaun Saor. "But find me the Unique Tale and what went before its beginning and what comes after its end, and I shall brighten the sword for you and show you the way to the Land of Mist. Go now, and search for the Unique Tale."

He went, and he had many far journeys, I can tell you, and he found no person who had any knowledge of the Unique Tale or who knew any way of coming to the Land of Mist. One twilight in a wood he saw a great bird flying toward him. It lighted on an old tree, and the King of Ireland's Son saw it was Laheen the Eagle.

"Are you still a friend to me, Eagle?" said the King's Son.

"I am still a friend to you, King's Son," said Laheen.

"Then tell me where I should go to get knowledge of the Unique Tale," said the King of Ireland's Son.

"The Unique Tale—I never heard of it at all," said Laheen the Eagle, changing from one leg to the other. "I am old," she said, shaking her wings, "and I never heard of the Unique Tale."

The King's Son looked and saw that Laheen was really old. Her neck was bare of feathers and her wings were gray. "Oh, if you are so old," said the King's Son, "and have gone to so many places, and do not know of the Unique Tale, to whom can I go to get knowledge of it?"

"Listen," said Laheen the Eagle, "there are five of us that are called the Five Ancient Ones of Ireland, and it is not known which one of the five is the oldest. There is myself, Laheen the Eagle; there is Blackfoot the Elk of Ben Gulban, there is the Crow of Achill, the Salmon of Assaroe, and the Old Woman of Beare. We do not know ourselves which of us is the oldest, but we know that we five are the most ancient of living things. I have never heard of the Unique Tale," said Laheen, "but maybe one of the other Ancients has heard of it."

"I will go to them," said the King's Son. "Tell me how I will find the Crow of Achill, the Elk of Ben Gulban, the Salmon of Assaroe, and the Old Woman of Beare— tell me how to go to them, Laheen the Eagle."

"You need not go to the Salmon of Assaroe," said the Eagle, "for the Salmon would not have heard any tale. I will get you means of finding the other three. Follow the stream now until you come to the river. Wait at the ford and I will fly to you there." Laheen the Eagle then shook her wings and flew slowly away. The King of Ireland's Son followed the stream until he came to the river —the River of the Ox it was.

IV

AND having come to the River of the Ox he sought the ford and waited there for Laheen the Eagle. When it was high noon he saw the shadow of the Eagle in the water of the ford. He looked up. Laheen let something fall into the shallows. It was a wheel. Then Laheen lighted on the rocks of a waterfall above the ford and spoke to the King of Ireland's Son.

"Son of King Connal," she said, "roll this wheel before you and follow it where it goes. It will bring you first where Blackfoot the Elk abides. Ask the Elk has he knowledge of the Unique Tale. If he has no knowledge of it start the wheel rolling again. It will bring you then where the Crow of Achill abides. If the Crow cannot tell you anything of the Unique Tale, let the wheel bring you to where the Old Woman of Beare lives. If she cannot tell you of the Unique Tale, I cannot give you any further help."

Laheen the Eagle then spread out her wings and rising above the mist of the waterfall flew away.

The King of Ireland's Son took the wheel out of the shallow water and set it rolling before him. It went on without his touching it again. Then he was going and ever going with the clear day going before him and the dark night coming behind him, going through scrubby fields and shaggy bog-lands, going up steep mountain sides and along bare mountain ridges, until at last he came to a high mound on a lonesome mountain. And as high as the mound and as lonesome as the mountain was the Elk that was standing there with wide, wide horns. The wheel ceased rolling.

"I am from Laheen the Eagle," said the King of Ireland's Son.

The Elk moved his wide-horned head and looked down at him. "And why have you come to me, son?" said the Elk.

"I came to ask if you had knowledge of the Unique Tale," said the King of Ireland's Son.

"I have no knowledge of the Unique Tale," said the Elk in a deep voice.

"And are you not Blackfoot the Elk of Ben Gulban, one of the five of the oldest creatures in the world?" said the King of Ireland's Son.

"I am the Elk of Ben Gulban," said Blackfoot, "and it may be that there is no creature in the world more ancient than I am. The Fianna hunted me with their hounds before the Sons of Milé came to the Island of Woods. If it was a Tale of Finn or Caelta or Goll, of Oscar or Oisin or Conan, I could tell it to you. But I know nothing of the Unique Tale."

Then Blackfoot the Elk of Ben Gulban turned his wide-horned head away and looked at the full old moon that was coming up in the sky. And the King of Ireland's Son took up the wheel and went to look for a shelter. He found a sheep-cote on the side of the mountain and lay down and slept between sheep.

V

WHEN the sun rose he lifted up the wheel and set it going before him. He was going and ever going down long hillsides and across spreading plains till he came to where old trees and treestumps were standing hardly close enough together to keep each other company. The wheel went through this ancient wood and stopped before a fallen oak-tree. And sitting on a branch of that oak, with a gray head bent and featherless wings gathered up to her neck was a crow.

"I come from Laheen the Eagle," said the King of Ireland's Son.

"What did you say?" said the Crow, opening one eye.

"I come from Laheen the Eagle," said the King of Ireland's Son again.

"Oh, from Laheen," said the Crow and closed her eye again.

"And I came to ask for knowledge of the Unique Tale," said the King of Ireland's Son.

"Laheen," said the Crow, "I remember Laheen the Eagle." Keeping her eyes shut, she laughed and laughed until she was utterly hoarse. "I remember Laheen the Eagle," she said again. "Laheen never found out what I did to her once. I stole the Crystal Egg out of her nest. Well, and how is Laheen the Eagle?" she said sharply, opening one eye.

"Laheen is well," said the King of Ireland's Son. "She sent me to ask if you had knowledge of the Unique Tale."

"I am older than Laheen," said the Crow. "I remember Paralon's People. The Salmon of Assaroe always said he was before Paralon's People. But never mind! Laheen can't say that. If I could only get the feathers to stay on my wings I'd pay Laheen a visit some day. How are Laheen and her bird flocks?"

"O Crow of Achill," said the King of Ireland's Son, "I was sent to ask if you had knowledge of the Unique Tale."

"The Unique Tale! No, I never heard of it," said the Crow. She gathered her wings up to her neck again and bent her gray head.

"Think, O Crow of Achill," said the King of Ireland's Son. "I will bring you the warmest wool for your nest."

"I never heard of the Unique Tale," said the Crow. "Tell Laheen I was asking for her." Nothing would rouse the Crow of Achill again. The King of Ireland's Son set the wheel rolling and followed it. Then he was going and ever going with the clear day before him and the dark night coming behind him. He came to a wide field where there were field-fares or ground larks in companies. He crossed it. He came to a plain of tall daisies where there were thousands of butterflies. He crossed it. He came to a field of buttercups where blue pigeons were feeding. He crossed it. He came to a field of flax in blue blossom. He crossed it and came to a smoke-blackened stone house deep sunk in the ground. The wheel stopped rolling before it and he went into the house.

An old woman was scated on the ground before the fire basting a goose. A rabbitskin cap was on her hairless head and there were no eyebrows on her face. Three strange birds were eating out of the pot—a cuckoo, a corncrake, and a swallow. "Come to the fire, gilly," said the old woman when she looked round.

"I am not a gilly, but the King of Ireland's Son," said he.

"Well, let that be. What do you want of me?"

"Are you the Old Woman of Beare?"

"I have been called the Old Woman of Beare since your fore-great-grandfather's time."

"How old are you, old mother?"

"I do not know. But do you see the three birds that are picking out of my pot? For two score years the swallow was coming to my house and building outside. Then he came and built inside. Then for three score years he was coming into my house to build here. Now he never goes across the sea at all. And do you see the corncrake? For five score years she was coming to the meadow outside. Then she began to run into the house to see what was happening here. For two score years she was running in and out. Then she stayed here altogether. Now she never goes across the sea at all. And do you see the cuckoo there? For seven score years she used to come to a tree that was outside and sing over her notes. Then when the tree was gone, she used to light on the roof of my house Then she used to come in to see herself in a looking glass. I do not know how many score years the cuckoo was going and coming, but I know it is many score years since she went across the sea."

"I went from Laheen the Eagle to Blackfoot the Elk, and from the Elk of Ben Gulban to the Crow of Achill, and from the Crow of Achill, I come to you to ask if you have knowledge of the Unique Tale."

"The Unique Tale, indeed," said the Old Woman of Beare. "One came to me only last night to tell me the Unique Tale. He is the young man who is counting the horns."

"What young man is he and what horns is he counting?"

"He is no King's Son, but a gilly—Gilly of the Goatskin he is called. He is counting the horns that are in two pits outside. When the horns are counted I will know the number of my half-years."

"How is that, old mother?"

"My father used to kill an ox every year on my birthday, and after my father's death, my servants, one after the other, used to kill an ox for me. The horns of the oxen were put into two pits, one on the right-hand side of the house and one on the left-hand side. If one knew the number of the horns one would know the number of my half-years, for every pair of horns goes to make a year of my life. Gilly of the Goatskin is counting the horns for me now, and when he finishes counting them I will let him tell the Unique Tale."

"But you must let me listen to the tale too, Old Woman of Beare."

"If you count the horns in one pit I will let you listen to the tale."

"Go outside then and count them."

The King of Ireland's Son went outside. He found on the right-hand side of the house a deep quarry pit. Round the edge of it were horns of all kinds, black horns and white horns, straight horns and crooked horns. And below in the pit he saw a young man digging for horns that were sunk in the ground. He had on a jacket made of the skin of a goat.

"Who are you?" said the young man in the quarry pit.

"I am the King of Ireland's Son. And who may you be?"

"Who I am I don't know," said the young man in the goatskin, "but they call me Gilly of the Goatskin. What have you come here for?"

"To get knowledge of the Unique Tale."

"And it was to tell the same Unique Tale that I came here myself. Why do you want to know the Unique Tale?"

"That would make a long story. Why do you want to tell it?"

"That would make a longer story. There is a quarry pit at the left-hand side of the house filled with horns and it must be your task to count them."

"I will count them," said the King of Ireland's Son. "But you will be finished before me. Do not tell the Old Woman of Beare the Tale until we both sit down together."

"If that suits you it will suit me," said Gilly of the Goatskin, and he began to dig again.

The King of Ireland's Son went to the left-hand side of the house. He found the quarry pit and went into it to count the horns that were there—black horns and white horns, straight horns and crooked horns. And now, while the King of Ireland's Son is in the quarry pit, I will tell you the adventures of Gilly—the Lad or the Servant—of the Goatskin, which adventures are written in "The Craneskin Book."

VI

HE never stirred out of the cradle till he was past twelve years of age, but lay there night and day, long days and short days; the only garment he ever put on was a goatskin; a hunter had once put it down on the floor beside his cradle and he reached out with his two hands, drew it in and put the goatskin on him. He got his name and his coat at the same time, for he was called ever afterwards "Gilly of the Goatskin."

But although he never stirred out of the cradle, Gilly of the Goatskin had ways of diverting himself. He used to shoot arrows with a bow out of the door of the house and hit a mark on a tree that was opposite him. *And where did he get the bow and arrows?* The bow fell down from the roof of the house and into the cradle. And as for arrows he used to make them out of the wands that the Hags brought in to make baskets with. But the Hags never saw him using the bow and sending off the arrows. All day they would be going along the streams gathering the willow wands for the baskets they made.

He knew nobody except the three Hags of the Long Teeth, and he had never heard the name of mother or father. Often, when she was peeling the wands with a black-handled knife, the Hag of the House used to tell Gilly of the Goatskin the troubles that were in store for him—danger from the sword and the spear and the knife, from water and fire, from the beasts of the earth and the birds of the air. She delighted to tell him about the evils that would befall him. And she used to laugh when she told him he was a humpback and that people would throw stones at him.

One day when the Hags were away gathering willow wands, Gilly turned the cradle over and lay under it. He wanted to see what they would do when they did not see him sitting up in the cradle. They came in. Gilly looked through a crack in the cradle and saw the Hags— they were old and crooked and had long teeth that came down below their chins.

"He's gone, he's gone, he's gone!" screamed the Hag of the House, when she did not see Gilly in the cradle.

"He's gone," said one of the long-toothed Hags. "I told you he would go away. Why didn't you cut out his heart yesterday, or the day before?"

"Mind what I tell you," said the other Hag of the Long Teeth. "Mind what I tell you. His father's son will grow into a powerful champion."

"Not he," said the Hag of the House, with great anger. "He'll never become a Champion. He's only a little hump-backed fellow with no weapons and with no garment but a goatskin."

"It would be better to kill him when he comes back," said the first of the Hags with the Long Teeth.

"And if he doesn't come back, tell the Giant Crom Duv," said the second.

Gilly of the Goatskin crept from under the cradle, put his bow resting on the bottom that was now turned uppermost, took up some of the rods that were on the floor and then shouted at the Hags. "Oh, if that's a hazel rod he has at his bow he will kill us all," they screamed out together.

He drew back the string, fired the willow rod and struck the middle Hag full on the breast. The three Hags

*"Oh, if that's a hazel rod he has at his bow
he will kill us all!"*

fell down on the ground. The pot that was always hanging over the fire turned itself upside down and the house
was filled with smoke. Gilly of the Goatskin, the bow in
his hand, sprang across the cradle, over the threshold
of the door, and out into the width and the height, the
length and the breadth, the gloom and the gleam of the
world.

VII

HE WAS out, as I have said, in the width and the height,
the length and the breadth, the gloom and the gleam
of the world. He fired arrows into the air. He leaped
over ditches, he rolled down hillsides, he raced over level
places until he came to what surprised him more than
all the things in the world—a river. He had never seen
such water before and he wondered to see it moving with
swiftness. "Where is it going?" said Gilly of the Goatskin. "Does it go on like that in the night as well as in
the day?" He ran by its side and shouted to the river. He
saw a wide-winged bird flying across it. It was the bird
that we call the crane or the heron. And as Gilly watched
the great winged thing he saw that it held a little animal in its claws. Gilly fired an arrow and the crane
dropped toward the ground. The little animal that was
in its claws fell down. The crane rose up again and flew
back across the river.

The little animal that had been in the claws of the
crane came to Gilly of the Goatskin. It was smaller than

the one-eyed cat that used to sit on the hearth of the Hag of the House. It kept its head up and was very bold-looking. "Good morning, Lad in the Goatskin," it said to Gilly, "you saved my life and I'm very thankful to you." "What are you?" said Gilly of the Goatskin. "I'm the Weasel. I'm the boldest and bravest creature in this country. I'm the lion of these parts, I am. And," said the Weasel, "I never served anyone before, but I'll be your servant for a quarter of a year. Tell me what way you're going and I'll go with you." "I'm going the way he's going," said Gilly, nodding toward the river, "and I'll keep beside him till he wants to turn back." "Oh, then you'll have to go a long way," said the Weasel, "but I'll go with you no matter how far you go." The Weasel walked by Gilly's side very bravely and very independently.

"Oh, look," said Gilly to the Weasel, "what is that that's in the water?"

The Weasel looked and saw a crystal egg in the shallows.

"It's an egg," said the Weasel, "I often eat one myself. I'll bring it up from the bottom to you. I'm good at carrying eggs."

The Weasel went into the water and put his mouth to the egg and tried to lift it. He could not move it. He tried to lift it with his paws as well as with his mouth; but this did not do either. He came up the bank then, and said to Gilly, "You'll think I'm a poor sort of a servant because I can't take an egg out of the water.

But if I can't win one way I'll win another way." He went into the reeds by the river and he said, "Hear me, frogs! There's a great army coming to take you out of the reeds and eat you red and raw." Then Gilly saw the queer frogs lifting up their heads, "Oh, what will we do, what will we do?" they cried to the Weasel. "There's only one thing to be done," said the Weasel. "You gather up all the pebbles in the bed of the river and we'll make a big wall on the bank to defend you." The frogs dived into the water at once and dragged up pebbles. Gilly and the Weasel piled them on the bank. Then three frogs carried up the Crystal Egg. The Weasel took it from them when they left it on the bank. Then he climbed a tree and cried out to the frogs, "The army is frightened and is running away." "Oh, thank you, thank you," said the frogs, "we'll never forget your goodness to us." Then they sat down in the marsh and told each other what a narrow escape they all had.

The Weasel gave Gilly the Crystal Egg. It was heavy and he carried it for a while in his hand. They went on. After a while said Gilly of the Goatskin, "The night's coming on and the river shows no sign of turning back. I wish there was a nice place to shelter us." No sooner did he say the word than he and the Weasel found themselves standing before the open door of a nice little house. They went in. A clear fire was burning on the hearth, an arm chair was before it, and a bed was made at the other side of the fire. "This is good," said Gilly, "and now I wish that we had something to eat." No sooner did he say the words than a table appeared with bread and meat, fruit, and wine on it. "Where do these fine things come from, I wonder," said Gilly of the Goatskin. "It's my belief," said the Weasel, "that all these things come to us on account of the egg you have in your hand. It's a magic egg." Gilly of the Goatskin put the egg on the table and wished that he might see himself as he had seen himself in the river. Nothing appeared. Then he took the egg in his hand and wished again. And then there was a looking glass on the wall before him, and he saw himself in it better than he had seen himself in the river. Gilly of the Goatskin knew that he had only to hold the Crystal Egg in his hand and wish, to get all he could think of.

VIII

GILLY OF THE GOATSKIN wished for wide windows in his house and he got them. He wished for a light within when there was darkness without, and he got a silver lamp that burned until he wished to sleep. He wished for the songs of birds and he had a blackbird singing upon his half-door, a lark over his chimney, a goldfinch and a green linnet within his window, and a shy wren in the evening singing from the top of his dresser. Then he wished to hear the conversation of the beasts and all the creatures of the fields and the wood and the mountain top came into his house.

The hare used to come in early in the morning. He was always the first visitor and he never remained long, and always while he was there he kept running up and down the house, and he generally ended his visit by jumping through the open window. The martens, the beautiful wild cats of the wood, came in to see Gilly once; they were very proud and told him nothing. The little black rabbits were very much impressed by the martens, and all the time the martens were there they stayed under the bed and the chairs. Two or three times the King of the Wood himself—the Boar of the Bristles and the Long Tusks—came to see Gilly; he used to push open the door and then stand in the middle of the floor grunting and grunting. Once he brought his wife with him, and six or seven of their little pigs that went running over the floor, with their ears hanging over their eyes, came with them too. The hedgehogs used to come, but they always made themselves disagreeable. They just lay down by the fire and snored, and when they wakened up they quarrelled with each other. Everybody said that the hedgehogs' children were very badly brought up and very badly provided for. The squirrels who were so clean and careful, and so fond of their children, thought the hedgehogs were very bad creatures indeed. "It is just like them to have dirty sticky thorns around them instead of nice clean fur," said the squirrel's wife. "But, my dear," said the squirrel, "every animal can't have fur." "How well," said she, "the rabbits have fur, though dear knows they're creatures of not much account. It's all just to let us see that they're some relation of that horrible, horrible boar that goes crashing and marching through the wood."

The deer never came into the house, and Gilly had a shed made for them outside. They would come into it and stay there for many nights and days, and Gilly used to go out and talk with them. They knew about far countries, and strange paths and passes, but they did not know so much about men and about the doings of other creatures as the Fox did.

The Fox used to come in the evening and stay until nearly morning whether Gilly fell asleep or kept awake. The Fox was a very good talker. He used to lie down at the hearth with his paws stretched out, and tell about this one and that one, and what she said and what he did. If the Fox came to see you, and if he was in good humor for talking, you would stay up all night to listen to him. I know I should. It was the Fox who told Gilly what the Crow of Achill did to Laheen the Eagle. She had stolen the Crystal Egg that Laheen was about to hatch—the Crystal Egg that the Crane had left on a bare rock. It was the Fox who told Gilly how the first cat came into the world. And it was the Fox who told Gilly about the generations of the eel. All I say is that it is a pity the Fox cannot be trusted, for a better one to talk and tell a story it would be hard to find. He was always picking up and eating things that had been left over—a potato roasting in the ashes, an apple left upon a plate, a piece of meat under a cover. Gilly did not grudge these things to Rory the Fox and he always left something in a bag for him to take home to the young foxes.

I had nearly forgotten to tell you about Gilly's friend,

the brave Weasel. He had made a home for himself under the roof. Sometimes he would go away for a day or so and he would never tell Gilly where he had been. When he was at home he made himself the doorkeeper of Gilly's house. If any of the creatures made themselves disagreeable by quarrelling amongst each other, or by being uncivil to Gilly, the Weasel would just walk over to them and look them in the eyes. Then that creature went away. Always he held his head up and if Gilly asked him for advice he would say three words, "Have no fear; have no fear."

One day Gilly wanted to have a bunch of cherries with his dinner, and he went to find the Crystal Egg so that he might wish for it. The Crystal Egg was not in the place he had left it. He called the Weasel and the two of them searched the house. The Crystal Egg was nowhere to be found. "One of the creatures has stolen the Egg," said the Weasel, "but whoever stole it I will make bring it back. I'll soon find out who did it." The Weasel walked up to every creature that came in, looked him or her in the eye and said, "Did you steal the Crystal Egg?" And every creature that came in said, "No, Little Lion, I didn't steal it." Next day they had examined every creature except the Fox. The Fox had not been in the night before nor the night before that again. He did not come in the evening they missed the Crystal Egg nor the evening after that evening. That night the Weasel said, "As sure as there are teeth in my head the Fox stole the Crystal Egg. As soon as there is light we'll search for him and make him give the Egg back to us."

IX

THE Weasel was right; it was Rory the Fox who had stolen Gilly's Crystal Egg. One night, just as he was leaving Gilly's house, the moon shone full upon the Crystal Egg. In the turn of a hand Rory the Fox had made a little spring and had taken the Egg in his mouth. Then he slipped out by the door as quick and as quiet as a leaf blown in the wind.

He couldn't help himself stealing the Egg, when the chance came. He had had a dream about it. He dreamt that the Egg had been hatched and that out of it had come the most toothsome bird that a Fox had ever taken by the neck. He snapped his teeth in his sleep when he dreamt of it. The Fox told his youngsters about the bird he had dreamt of—a bird as big as a goose and so fat on the neck and the breast that it could hardly stir from sitting. The youngsters had smacked their lips and snapped their teeth. Every time he came home now they used to say to him—"Father, have you brought us the Boobrie Bird?" No wonder that his eyes used to turn to the Crystal Egg when he sat in Gilly's house. And then because the moon shone on it just as he was leaving, and because he knew that Gilly's back was turned, he could not keep himself from making a little spring and taking the Crystal Egg softly in his mouth.

He went amongst the dark, dark trees with the soft and easy trot of a Fox. He knew well what he should

do with the Egg. He had dreamt that it had been hatched
by the Spae-Woman's old rheumatic goose. This goose
was called Old Mother Hatchie and the Fox had never
carried her off because he knew she was always hatching
out goslings for his table. He went through the trees and
across the fields toward the Spae-Woman's house.

The Spae-Woman lived by telling people their fortunes and reading them their dreams. That is why she
was called the Spae-Woman. The people gave her goods
for telling them their dreams and fortunes and she left
her land and stock to whatever chanced. The fences of
her fields were broken and rotted. Her hens had been
carried off by the Fox. Her goat had gone wild. She had
neither ox nor ass nor sheep nor pig. The Fox went
through her fence now as lightning would go through
a gooseberry bush and he came out before her barn.
There was a hole in the barn door and he went through
that. And in the northwest corner of the barn, he saw
Old Mother Hatchie sitting on a nest of straw and he
knew that there was a clutch of eggs under her. She
cackled when she saw the Fox on the floor of the barn
but she never stirred off the nest. Rory left what was in
his mouth on the ground. Old Mother Hatchie put her
head on one side and looked at the Egg that was clear
in the full moonlight.

"This egg, Mistress Hatchie," said Rory the Fox, "is
from the Hen-wife of the Queen of Ireland. The Queen
asked the Hen-wife to ask me to leave it with you. She
thinks there's no bird in the world but yourself that is

worthy to hatch it and to rear the gosling that comes out of it."

"That's right, that's right," said Mother Hatchie. "Put it here, put it here." She lifted her wing and the Fox put the Crystal Egg into the brood-nest.

He went out of the barn, crossed the field again, and went amongst the dark, dark trees. He went along slowly now for he began to think that Gilly might find out who stole the Crystal Egg and be vexed with him. Then he thought of the Weasel. The Fox began to think he might be sorry for himself if the Weasel was set on his track.

Rory did not go to Gilly's house the next night nor the night after. The third night, as he was going home from a ramble, the Owl hooted at him. "Why do you hoot at me, Big Moth?" said the Fox stopping in his trot. (He always called the Owl "Big Moth" to pretend that he thought she wasn't a bird at all, but a moth. He made this pretence because he was annoyed that he could never get an owl to eat). "Why do you hoot at me, Big Moth?" said he. "The Weasel's going to have your bones for his stepping-stones and your blood for his morning dram," said the Owl balefully as she went amongst the dark, dark trees. The Fox stopped long to consider. Then he went to his burrow and told his youngsters they would have to move house. He had them stirring at the first light. He gave them a frog each for their breakfast and took them across the country. They came to a burrow that Old-Fellow Badger had just left and Rory the Fox brought his youngsters into it and told them that it would be their new house.

X

THE evening after when Rory the Fox was taking his nap he heard one of his youngsters give a sharp cry. They were playing outside the burrow. He looked out and he saw that his three youngsters were afraid of something that was between them and the burrow. He looked again and saw the Weasel.

"Ahem," said Rory the Fox, "and how are we this morning?"

The Weasel had marked one of Rory's youngsters for attack. Although Rory spoke, he never took his eyes off the youngster he had marked.

"My dear friend," said the Fox, "I was just going to say—if you are looking for anything, perhaps I could tell you where it might be found."

"Crystal Egg," said the Weasel without ever taking away his blood-thirsty gaze from Rory's youngster.

"Oh, the Crystal Egg," said Rory the Fox. "Yes, to be sure. I could bring you at once to the place where the Crystal Egg is." He came out of the burrow and saw Gilly standing on the bank behind.

"I think it is time for my children to go back to their burrow," said Rory the Fox. "Please excuse them, my friends." The Weasel took his eyes off the youngster he had marked and the three little foxes scampered into the burrow.

"This way, friends," said the Fox, and he started off towards the Spae-Woman's house with the light and easy trot of a fox. Gilly and the Weasel went behind him. They crossed a field of flax, a field of hemp, and a field of barley. They came to the broken fence before the Spae-Woman's house, and in front of the house they saw the Spae-Woman herself and she was crying and crying.

The Fox hid behind the fence, the Weasel climbed up on the ditch and Gilly himself went to the woman.

"What ails you at all?" said Gilly to her.

"My goose—the only fowl left to me has been taken by robbers."

"Ask her where the clutch of eggs is that the goose was hatching," said Rory the Fox anxiously, putting his head over the fence.

"And where is the clutch of eggs, ma'am, that your goose was hatching?"

"The robbers took the nest with the goose and the eggs with the nest," said the Spae-Woman.

"And the Crystal Egg was with the other eggs," said the Fox to Gilly. He said no more. He make a quick turn and got clear away before the Weasel could spring on him. He ran back to his burrow. He told the little foxes they must change houses again. That night they lay in a wood and at the first light they crossed water and went to live on an island where the Weasel never came.

"Where did the robbers go with the goose, the nest, and the eggs?" said Gilly of the Goatskin.

"They went to the river," said the Spae-Woman. "I followed them every inch of the way. They got into a boat and they hoisted their sails. They rowed and they rowed, so that the hard gravel of the bottom was brought to the top, and the froth of the top was driven down to the bottom of the river. And wherever they are," said the Spae-Woman, "they are far from us now."

"Will you come with me?" said Gilly to the Weasel, "we will track them down and take back the Crystal Egg."

"I engaged myself to be with you for a quarter of a year," said the Weasel, "and the three months are up now, Gilly. Winter is coming on and I must see to my own affairs."

"Then goodby, Weasel," said Gilly. "I will search for the Crystal Egg myself. But first I must ask the woman to let me rest in the house and to give me some provision for my journey."

The Weasel looked up into Gilly's face and said goodby to him. Then Gilly followed the Spae-Woman into her house. "Ocone," she was saying to herself, "my dream told me I was to lose my poor goose, and still I never did anything to make it hard for the robbers to take her from me."

XI

WELL, in the Spae-Woman's house he stayed for three-quarters of a year. He often went in search of the robbers who had taken the Crystal Egg with the Spae-Woman's goose, but no trace of them nor their booty could he ever find. He met birds and beasts who were his friends, but he could not have speech with them without the Egg that let him have anything he wished. He did work for the Spae-Woman—fixed her fences and repaired her barn and brought *brosna* for her fire every evening from the wood. At night, before he went to sleep, the Spae-Woman used to tell him her dreams of the night before and tell him about the people who had come to her house to have their fortunes told.

One Monday morning she said to him, "I have had an inlook, son of my heart, and I know that my gossip, the Churl of the Townland of Mischance, is going to come and take you into his service."

"And what sort of a man is your gossip, the Churl of the Townland of Mischance?" Gilly asked.

"An unkind man. Two youths who served me he took away, one after the other, and miserable are they made by what he did to them. I'm in dread of your being brought to the Townland of Mischance."

"Why are you in dread of it, Spae-Woman?" said Gilly. "Sure, I'll be glad enough to see the world."

"That's what the other two youths said," said the Spae-Woman. "Now I'll tell you what my gossip, the Churl of the Townland of Mischance does: he makes a bargain with the youth that goes into his service, telling him he will give him a guinea, a groat, and a tester for his three months' service. And he tells the youth that if he says he is sorry for the bargain he must lose his wages and part with a strip of his skin, an inch wide, from his neck to his heel. Oh, he is an unkind man, my gossip, the Churl of the Townland of Mischance."

"And is there no way to get the better of him?" asked Gilly.

"There is, but it is a hard way," said the Spae-Woman. "If one could make him say that he, the master, is sorry for the bargain, the Churl himself would lose a strip of his skin an inch wide from his neck to his heel, and would have to pay full wages no matter how short a time the youth served him."

"It's a bargain anyway," said Gilly, "and if he comes I'll take service with the Churl of the Townland of Mischance."

The first wet day that came brought the Churl of the Townland of Mischance. He rode on a bob-tailed, big-headed, spavined, and spotted horse. He carried an ash-plant in his hand to flog the horse and to strike at the dogs that crossed his way. He had blue lips, eyes looking crossways, and eyebrows like a furze bush. He had a bag before him filled with boiled pigs' feet. Now when he rode up to the house, he had a pig's foot to his mouth and was eating. He got down off the bob-tailed, big-headed, spavined, and spotted horse, and came in.

"I heard there was a young fellow at your house and I want him to take service with me," said he to the Spae-Woman.

He rode on a bob-tailed, big-headed,
spavined, and spotted horse.

"If the bargain is a good one I'll take service with you," said Gilly.

"All right, my lad," said the Churl. "Here is the bargain, and it's as fair as fair can be. I'll give you a guinea, a groat, and a tester for your three months' work with me."

"I believe it's good wages," said Gilly.

"It is. Howsoever, if you ever say you are sorry you made the bargain you will lose your wages, and besides that you will lose a strip of your skin an inch wide from your neck to your heel. I have to put that in or I'd never get work done for me at all. The serving boys are always saying 'I can't do that,' and 'I'm sorry I made the bargain with you.'"

"And if you say you're sorry you made the bargain?"

"Oh, then I'll have to lose a strip of my skin an inch wide from my neck to my heel, and besides that I'll have to give you full wages no matter how short a time you served me."

"Well, if that suits you it will suit me," said Gilly of the Goatskin.

"Then walk beside my horse and we'll get back to the Townland of Mischance tonight," said the Churl. Then he swished his ash-plant toward Gilly and ordered him to get ready. The Spae-Woman wiped the tears from her face with her apron, gave Gilly a cake with her blessing, and he started off with the Churl for the Townland of Mischance.

XII

WHAT did Gilly of the Goatskin do in the Town-land of Mischance? He got up early and went to bed late: he was kept digging, delving, and ditching until he was so tired that he could go to sleep in a furze bush: he ate a breakfast that left him hungry five hours before dinnertime, and he ate a dinner that made it seem long until suppertime. If he complained the Churl would say, "Well, then you are sorry for your bargain," and Gilly would say, "No," rather than lose the wages he had earned and a strip of his skin into the bargain.

One day the Churl said to him, "Go into the town for salt for my supper, take the short way across the pasture-field, and be sure not to let the grass grow under your feet." "All right, master," said Gilly. "Maybe you would bring me my coat out of the house so that I needn't make two journeys." The Churl went into the house for Gilly's coat. When he came back he found Gilly standing in the nice grass of the pasture-field lighting a wisp of hay. "What are you doing that for?" said the Churl to him. "To burn the grass on the pasture-field," said Gilly. "To burn the grass on my pasture-field, you villain—the grass that is for my good race-horse's feeding! What do you mean, at all?" "Sure, you told me not to let the grass grow under my feet," said Gilly. "Doesn't the world know that the grass is growing every minute, and how will I prevent it from growing under my feet if I don't burn it?" With that he stooped down to put the lighted hay to the grass of the pasture-field. "Stop, stop," said the Churl, "I meant that you were to go to the town, without loitering on the way." "Well, it's a pity you didn't speak more clearly," said Gilly, "for now the grass is a-fire." The Churl had to stamp on the grass to put the fire out. He burnt his shins, and that made him very angry. "O you fool," said he to Gilly, "I'm sorry—" "Are you sorry for the bargain you made with me, Master?" "No. I was going to say I was sorry I hadn't made my meaning clear to you. Go now to the town and bring me back salt for my supper as quickly as you can."

After that the Churl was very careful when he gave Gilly an order to speak to him very exactly. This became a great trouble to him, for the people in the Townland of Mischance used always to say, "Don't let the grass grow under your feet," when they meant "Make haste," and "Don't be there until you're back," when they meant "Go quickly," and "Come with horses' legs," when they meant "Come with great speed." He became tired of speaking to Gilly by the letter, so he made up his mind to give him an order that could not be carried out, so that he might have a chance of sending him away without the wages he had earned.

One Monday morning he called Gilly to the door of the house and said to him, "Take this sheepskin to the market and bring me back the price of it and the skin." "Very well, Master," said Gilly. He put the skin across his arm and went toward the town. The people on the road said to him, "What do you want for the sheepskin, young fellow?" "I want the skin and the price of it," Gilly said. The people laughed at him and said, "You're going to give yourself a long journey, young fellow."

He went through the market asking for the skin and the price of it. Everyone joked about him. He went into the markethouse and came to a woman who was buying things that no one else would buy. "What do you want, youth?" said she. "The price of the skin and the skin itself," said Gilly. She took the skin from him and plucked the wool out of it. She put the wool in her bag and put the skin back on the board. "There's the skin," said she, "and here's the price of it." She left three groats and a tester on top of the skin.

The Churl had finished his supper when Gilly came into the house. "Well, Master, I've come back to you," said Gilly. "Did you bring me the price of it and the skin itself?" said the Churl. "There is the skin," said Gilly, putting on the table the sheepskin with the wool plucked out of it. "And here's the price of it—three groats and a tester," said he, leaving the money on top of the skin.

After that the Churl of the Townland of Mischance began to be afraid that Gilly of the Goatskin would be too wise for him, and would get away at the end of the three months with his wages, a guinea, a groat, and a tester, in his fist. This thought made the Churl very downcast, because, for many months now, he had got hard labor out of his serving-boys, without giving them a single cross for wages.

XIII

THE day after Christmas the Churl said to Gilly, "This is Saint Stephen's Day. I'm going to such a man's barn to see the mummers perform a play. Foolish people give these idle fellows money for playing, but I won't do any such thing as that. I'll see something of what they are doing, drink a few glasses, and get away before they start collecting money from the people that are watching them. They call this collection their dues, no less."

"And what can I do for you, Master?" said Gilly.

"Run into the barn at midnight and shout out, 'Master, Master, your mill is on fire.' That will give me an excuse for running out. Do you understand now what I want you to do?"

"I understand, Master."

The Churl put on his coat and took his stick in his hand. "Mind what I've said to you," said he. "Don't be a minute later than midnight. Be sure to come in with a great rush—come in with horse's legs—do you understand me?"

"I understand you, Master," said Gilly.

The mummers were dancing before they began the play when the Churl came into the barn. "That's a rich man," said one of them to another. "We must see that he puts a good handful into our bag." The Churl sat on the bench with the farmer who had a score of cows, with the blacksmith who shod the King's horses, and with the merchant who had been in foreign parts and who wore big silver rings in his ears. Half the people who were there I could not tell you, but there were there—

Biddie Early
Tatter-Jack Walsh
Aunt Jug
Lundy Foot
Matt the Thresher
Nora Criona
Conan Maol, and
Shaun the Omadhaun.

Some said that the King of Ireland's Son was there too. The play was

"The Unicorn from the Stars"

The mummers did it very well although they had no one to take the part of the Unicorn.

They were in the middle of the play when Gilly of the Goatskin rushed into the barn. "Master, master," he shouted, "your mill—your mill is on fire." The Churl stood up, and then put his glass to his head and drained what was in it. "Make way for me, good people," said he. "Let me out of this, good people."

Some people near the door began to talk of what Gilly held in his hands. "What have you there, my servant?" said the Churl. "A pair of horse's legs, Master. I could only carry two of them."

The Churl caught Gilly by the throat. "A pair of horse's legs," said he. "Where did you get a pair of horse's legs?"

"Off a horse," said Gilly. "I had trouble in cutting them off. Bad cess to you for telling me to come here with horse's legs."

"And whose horse did you cut the legs off?"

"Your own, Master. You wouldn't have liked me to cut the legs off any other person's horse. And I thought your race-horse's legs would be the most suitable to cut off."

The mummers and the people were gathered round them and they saw the Churl's face get black with vexation.

"O my misfortune, that ever I met with you," said the Churl.

"Are you sorry for your bargain, Master?" said Gilly.

"Sorry—I'll be sorry every day and night of my life for it," said the Churl.

"You hear what my Master says, good people," said Gilly.

"Aye, sure. He says he's sorry for the bargain he made with you," said some of the people.

"Then," said Gilly, "strip him and put him across

the bench until I cut a strip of his skin an inch wide from his neck to his heel."

None of the people would consent to do that. "Well, I'll tell you something that will make you consent," said Gilly. "This man made two poor servant-boys work for him, paid them no wages, and took a strip of their skin, so that they are sick and sore to this day. Will that make you strip him and put him across the bench?"

"No," said some of the people.

"He ordered me to come here tonight and to shout 'Master, master, your mill is on fire,' so that he might be able to leave without paying the mummers their dues. His mill is not on fire at all."

"Strip him," said the first mummer.

"Put him across the bench," said another.

"Here's a skinner's knife for you," said a third.

The mummers seized the Churl, stripped him and put him across the bench. Gilly took the knife and began to sharpen it on the ground.

"Have mercy on me," said the Churl.

"You did not have mercy on the other two poor servant-boys," said Gilly.

"I'll give you your wages in full."

"That's not enough."

"I'll give you double wages to give to the other servant-boys."

"And will you pay the mummers' dues for all the people here?"

"No, no, no. I can't do that."

"Stretch out your neck then until I mark the place where I shall begin to cut the skin."

"Don't put the knife to me. I'll pay the dues for all," said the Churl.

"You heard what he said," said Gilly to the people. "He will pay me wages in full, give me double wages to hand to the servant-boys he has injured, and pay the mummers' dues for everyone."

"We heard him say that," said the people.

"Stand up and dress yourself," said Gilly to the Churl. "What do I want with a strip of your skin? But I hope all here will go home with you and stand in your house until you have paid all the money that's claimed from you."

"We'll go home with him," said the mummers.

"We'll stand on his floor until he has paid all the money he has agreed to pay," said the others.

"And now I must tell you, neighbors," said Gilly, "that I never cut the legs of a living horse—neither his horse nor anyone else's. This pair was taken off a poor dead horse by the skinners that were cutting it up."

Well, they all went to the Churl's house and there they stayed until he opened his stone chest and took out his money box and paid to the mummers the dues of all the people with sixpence over, and paid Gilly his wages in full, one guinea, one groat, and a tester, and handed him double wages to give to each of the servant-boys he had injured. Gilly took the money and left the house of the Churl of the Townland of Mischance, and the people and the mummers went to the road with him, and cheered him as we went on his way.

XIV

So, without hap or mishap, Gilly came again to the house of the Spae-Woman. She was sitting at her door-step grinding corn with a quern when he came before her. She cried over him, not believing that he had come safe from the Townland of Mischance. And as long as he was with her she spoke to him of his "poor back."

He stayed with her for two seasons. He mended her fences and he cleaned her spring-well; he ground her corn and he brought back her swarm of bees; he trained a dog to chase the crows out of her field; he had the ass shod, the sheep washed, and the goat spancelled. The Spae-Woman was much beholden to him for all he did for her, and one day she said to him, "Gilly of the Goat-skin you are called, but another name is due to you now." "And who will give me another name?" said Gilly of the Goatskin. "Who'll give it to you? Who but the Old Woman of Beare," said the Spae-Woman.

The next day she said to him, "I had a dream last night, and I know now what you are to do. You must go now to the Old Woman of Beare for the name that is due to you. And before she gives it to you, you must tell her and whoever else is in her house as much as you know of the Unique Tale."

"But I know nothing at all of the Unique Tale," said Gilly of the Goatskin.

"There is always a blank before a .beginning," said the Spae-Woman. "This evening, when I am grinding the corn at the quern I shall tell you the Unique Tale."

That evening when she sat at the doorstep of her house and when the sun was setting behind the elder-bushes the Spae-Woman told Gilly the third part of the Unique Tale. Then she baked a cake and killed a cock for him and told him to start on the morrow's morning for the house of the Old Woman of Beare.

Well, he started off in the morning bright and early, leaving good health with the Spae-Woman behind him, and away he went, crossing high hills, passing low dales, and keeping on his way without halt or rest, the clear day going and the dark night coming, taking lodgings each evening wherever he found them, and at last he came to the house of the Old Woman of Beare.

He went into the house and found her making marks in the ashes of her fire while her cuckoo, her corn-crake, and her swallow were picking grains off the table.

"And what can I do for you, good youth?" said the Old Woman of Beare.

"Give me a name," said Gilly, "and listen to the story I have to tell you."

"That I will not," said the Old Woman of Beare, "until you have done a task for me."

"What task can I do for you?" said Gilly of the Goatskin.

"I would know," said she, "which of us four is the

oldest creature in the world—myself or Laheen the Eagle, Blackfoot the Elk or the Crow of Achill—I leave the Salmon of Assaroe out of account altogether."

"And how can a youth like me help you to know that?" said Gilly of the Goatskin.

"An ox was killed on the day I was born and on every one of my birthdays afterwards. The horns of the oxen are in two quarries outside. You must count them and tell me how much half of them amounts to and then I shall know my age."

"That I'll do if you feed me and give me shelter," said Gilly of the Goatskin.

"Eat as you like," said the Old Woman of Beare. She pushed him a loaf of bread and a bottle of water. When he cut a slice of the loaf it was just as if nothing had been cut off, and when he took a cupful out of the bottle it was as if no water had been taken out of it at all. When he had drunk and eaten he left the complete loaf and the full bottle of water on the shelf, went outside and began to count the horns on the right-hand side.

On the second day a strange youth came to him and saluted him, and then went to count the horns in the quarry on the left-hand side. This youth was none other than the King of Ireland's Son.

On the third day they had the horns all counted. Then Gilly of the Goatskin and the King of Ireland's Son met together under a bush. "How many horns have you counted?" said the King of Ireland's Son. "So many," said Gilly of the Goatskin. "And how many horns have you counted?" "So many," said the King of Ireland's Son.

Just as they were adding the two numbers together they both heard sounds in the air—they were like the sounds that Bards make chanting their verses. And when they looked up they saw a swan flying round and round above them. And the swan chanted the story of the coming of the Milesians to Eirinn, and as the two youths listened they forgot the number of horns they had counted. And when the swan had flown away they looked at each other and as they were hungry they went into the house and ate slices of the unwasted loaf and drank cupfuls out of the inexhaustible bottle. Then the Old Woman of Beare wakened up and asked them to tell her the number of her years.

"We cannot tell you although we counted all the horns," said the King of Ireland's Son, "for just as we were putting the numbers together a swan sang to us and we forgot the number we had counted."

"You didn't do your task rightly," she said, "but as I promised to give this youth a name and to listen to the story he had to tell, I shall have to let it be. You may tell the story now, Gilly of the Goatskin."

They sat at the fire, and while the Old Woman of Beare spun threads on a very ancient spindle, and while the corncrake, the cuckoo, and the swallow picked up grains and murmured to themselves, Gilly of the Goatskin told them the Unique Tale. And the story as Gilly of the Goatskin told it follows this.—

THE UNIQUE TALE

A KING and a Queen were walking one day by the
blue pool in their domain. The swan had come
to the blue pool, and the bright yellow flowers of the
broom were above the water. "Och," said the Queen,
"if I might have a daughter that would show such
colors—the blue of the pool in her eyes, the bright yellow of the broom in her hair, and the white of the
swan in her skin—I would let my seven sons go with
the wild geese." "Hush," said the King. "You ask for
a doom, and it may be sent you." A shivering came
upon the Queen. They went back to the Castle, and
that evening the nurse told them that a gray man had
passed in a circle round her seven sons saying, "If it

be as your mother desired, let it be as she has said."

Well, before the broom blossomed again and before the swan came to the blue pool, a child was born to the Queen. It was a girl. The King was sitting with his seven sons when the women came to tell him of the new birth. "O my sons," said he, "may ye be with me all my life." But his sons moved from him as he said it. Out through the door they went, and up the mound that was before the door. There they changed into gray wild geese, and the seven flew toward the empty hills.

No councillor that the King consulted could help to win them back again, and no hunter that he sent through the country could gain tale or tidings of them. The King and Queen were left with one child only, the girl just born. They called her "Sheen," a word that means "Storm," because her coming was a storm that swept away her seven brothers. The Queen died, my hearers. Then little Sheen was forgotten by her father, and she was reared and companioned by the servants of the house.

One day, when she was the age her eldest brother was when he was changed from his human form, Sheen went with Mor, the Woodman's daughter, and Siav, the basketmaker's fosterchild, to gather berries in the wood. Going here and there she got separated from Siav and Mor. She came to a place where there were lots of berries and went step after step to pick them. Her feet went down in a marsh. She cried to Mor and Siav, but no answers came from them. She cried and cried again. Her cries startled seven wild geese that rose up and flew round her. "Save me," she cried to them. Then one of the wild geese spoke to her. "Anyone but a girl we would save from the marsh, but such a one we cannot save, because it was a girl who lost us our human forms and the loving companionship of our father." Then Sheen knew—for the servants had often told her the story—that it was one of her seven brothers who spoke. "Since ever I knew of it," said she, "the whole of my trouble has been that I was the cause of your losing your human form and the companionship of our father who is now called the Lonely King. Believe me," said she, "that I would have striven and striven to win you back." There was so much feeling in her voice that her seven brothers, although they had been hardened by thinking about their misfortune, were touched at their hearts and they flew down to help her. They bore up her arms, they caught at her shoulders, they raised up her feet. They carried her beyond the marsh. Then she knelt down and cried to them, "O my brothers dear, is there anything I can do to restore you to your human forms?" "There is," said the first of the seven wild geese. She begged them to tell it to her. "It's a long and a tiresome labor we would put on you," said one. "If you would gather the light down that grows on the bogs with your own hands," said another, "and if you spun that down into threads, and wove the threads into a cloth, and sewed the cloth into a shirt, and did that over and over again until you had made seven shirts for us, all that time without laughing or crying or saying a word, you could save us. One shirt you could weave and spin and sew in a year. And it would not be until the seven shirts were put upon us that the human form would be restored to each of us." "I would be glad to do all that," said Sheen, "and I would cry no tear, laugh no laugh, and say no word all the time I was doing this task."

Then said the eldest brother, "The marsh is between you and our father's house, and between you and the companions who were with you today. If you would do the task that would restore us to our human forms, it were best you did not go back. Beyond the trees is the house of a lone woman, and there you may live until your task is finished." The seven wild geese then flew back to the marsh, and Sheen went to the house beyond the trees. The Spae-Woman lived there. She took Sheen to be a dumb girl, and she gave her food and shelter for the services she did—bringing water from the well in the daytime and grinding corn at the quern at dusk. She had the rest of the day and night for her own task. She gathered the bog-down between noon and sunset and spun the thread at night. When she had lengths of thread spun she began to weave them on the loom. At the end of a year she had the first shirt made. In another year she made the second, then the third, then the fourth, the fifth, and the sixth. And all the time she said no word, laughed no laugh, and cried no tear.

She was gathering the bog-down for the seventh and last shirt. Once she went abroad on a day when the snow was melted and she felt her footsteps light. Hundreds of birds were on the ground eating plentifully and calling to one another. Sheen could hardly keep from her mouth the song that was in her mind. She would sing and laugh and talk when the last thread was spun and woven, when the last stitch was sewn, and when the shirts of bog-down she had made in silence would have brought back her brothers to their own human forms. She gathered the scarce heads of the cannavan or bog-down with one hand, while she held the other hand to her lips.

Something dropped down at her feet. It was a white grouse and it remained cowering on the ground. Sheen looked up and she saw a hawk above. And when she looked round she saw a man coming across the bog. The hawk flew toward him and lighted on his shoulder.

Sheen held the white grouse to her breast. The man came near to her and spoke to her and his voice made her stand. He wore the dress of a hunter. His face was brown and lean and his eyes were bright-blue like gentian-flowers. No word did Sheen say to him and he passed on with the hawk on his shoulder. Then with the grouse held at her breast she went back to the Spae-Woman's house.

That night when she spun her thread she thought of the blue-eyed, brown-faced man. Would any of her brothers be like him, she wondered, when they were restored to their human shapes. She fed the white grouse with grains of corn and left it to rest in the

window-niche above her bed. And then she lay awake
and tried to know the meaning in the song the Spae-
Woman sang when she sat spinning wool in the
chimney corner—

> You would not slumber
> If laid at my breast!
> Little sister,
> I'll rock you to rest!
>
> The flood on the river beats
> The swan from its nest!
> You would not slumber
> If laid at my breast!
>
> The rain-drops encumber
> The hawthorn's crest:
> My thoughts have no number:
> You would not slumber
> If laid at my breast,
> Little sister,
> I'll rock you to rest.

She passed the night between sleeping and waking,
and when the light grew she saw the white grouse
crouching against the window opening. She opened the
door and stepped outside to let the grouse fly from
her hands.

And there, on the ground before her was a sword!
Sheen knew it to be the sword of the man she had seen
yesterday, and she knew the man had been before the
door in the nighttime. She knelt on the ground to look

at the bright blue blade. O my listeners, if I was there I was in the crows that flew down heavily and cawed as they picked up something that pleased them, in the wood-cushats that cooed in the trees, in the small birds that quarreled in the thatch of the house, and in the breeze that blew round—the first breeze of the day.

The Spae-Woman came outside and saw what Sheen was looking at—the sword on the ground. "It is wrought with cunning that only the smiths of Kings possess," she said. She took the sword and hung it on the branch of a tree so that the dews of the ground might not rust it. "I think the one who owns it is the stranger who is seen in the wild places hereabouts—the man whom the neighbors call the Hunter-King," she said to Sheen.

On another day Sheen went to gather bog-down. This time she crossed the river by the steppingstones and went into a country where there were many cattle. She stood wondering at their numbers and wishing that such a cow and such a calf might belong to the Spae-Woman. Then the next thing she saw was two black horses striving with each other. They showed their teeth at each other and bit and kicked. Then they came racing toward her. "Oh," said Sheen to herself, "they are Breogan's wild stallions." She ran, but the horses were able to make circles round her. "Breogan's wild stallions," said she, "they will rush in and trample me to death." Then she heard someone shouting commands to the horses. She saw a man strike one of the stallions with a staff, making him rear high. She saw him make the other stand with the command that was in his voice. She ran to the river, but she slipped on the steppingstones; she fell down and she felt the water flowing upon her. The man came and lifting her up carried her to her own side of the river. Across the bog he carried her, and when she looked at him she saw the lean face and eyes blue like gentian-flowers— she saw the face of the man who was called the Hunter-King. He left her on the ground when they passed the bog, and she went on her way without speaking.

Nothing of this no more than of anything else that happened to her, or anything that she thought of, did Sheen tell the Spae-Woman. But she wished and she wished that the Hunter-King might come past while there was a light in the house and step within and talk to the Spae-Woman, so that she herself, while spinning the thread, could hear his voice and listen to the things he talked about. She often stood at the door and watched across the bog to see if anything was coming to her.

A neighbor woman came across the door-step one evening and Sheen went into the house after her, for she felt that something was going to be told. There was a dead man in a house. He had been found in the wood. He was known as the Hunter-King. Sheen stood at her bed and heard what the neighbor woman said.

The Hunter-King was being waked in the neighbor-woman's house, and her eldest daughter had been the corpse-watcher the first night. In the morning they found that the girl's hand had been withered. The woman's second daughter was the corpse-watcher the second night and her right hand had been left trembling. This was the third and last night that the Hunter-King would be waked, and tonight there was no one to watch his corpse.

Sheen thought that nothing would ever happen in the world again, now that the Hunter-King was dead. She thought that there was no loneliness so great as that of his corpse with no one to watch it on the last strange night it would be above ground. The neighbor woman went from the Spae-Woman and Sheen went after her. She was standing on the doorstep of her house. "Oh, colleen," said the neighbor woman, "I am wanting a girl to watch a corpse in my house tonight—the third and the last night for watching. Will you watch and I will give you a comb for your hair?" Sheen showed that she would serve the woman and she went into the wake-house. At first she was afraid to look at the bed. Then she went over and saw the Hunter-King with his face still, his eyes closed down, and the plate of salt on his breast. His gray gaunt hound was stretched across his feet.

The woman and her daughters lighted candles and placed them in the window recesses and at the head of the corpse. Then they went into their dormer-room and left Sheen to her watching. She sat at the fire and made one fagot after another blaze up. She had brought her basket of bog-down and she began to spin a thread upon the neighbor-woman's wheel.

She finished the thread and put it round her neck. Then she began to search for more candles so that she might be able to light one, as another went out. But as she rose up all the candles went out all at once. The hound started from the foot of the bed. Then she saw the corpse sitting up stiffly in the place where it had been laid.

Something in Sheen overcame her dread, and she went over to the corpse and took the salt that was on its breast and put it on its lips. Then a voice came from between the lips. "Fair Maid," said the voice, "have you the courage to follow me? The others failed me and they have been stricken. Are you faithful?" "I will follow you," said Sheen. "Then," said the corpse, "put your hands on my shoulders and come with me. I must go over the Quaking Bog, and through the Burning Forest, and across the Icy Sea." Sheen put her hands on his shoulders. A storm came and they were swept through the roof of the house. They were carried through the night. Down they came on the ground and the dead man sprang away from Sheen. She went to follow him and found her feet upon a shaking sod. They were on the Quaking Bog, she knew. The corpse of the Hunter-King went ahead and she knew that she must keep it in sight. He went swiftly. The sod went under her feet and she was in the watery mud. She

She saw the corpse sitting up stiffly.

struggled out and jumped over a pool that was hidden with heather. All the time she was in dread that the figure that went before her so quickly would be lost to her. She sank and she struggled and she sprang across pools and morasses. All the time what had been the corpse of the Hunter-King went before her.

Then she saw fires against the sky and she knew they were coming to the Burning Forest. The figure before her sprang across a ditch and went into the forest. Sheen sprang across it too. Burning branches fell across her path as she went on. Hot winds burnt her face. Flames dazzled and smoke dazed her. But the figure before her went straight on and Sheen went straight on too.

The forest ended on a cliff. Below was the sea. The figure before her dived down and Sheen dived too. The cold chilled her to the marrow. She thought the chill would drive the life out of her. But she saw the head of one swimming before her and she swam on.

And then they were on land again. "Fair Maid," said the corpse of the Hunter-King, "put your hands on my shoulders again." She put her hands on his shoulders. A storm came and swept them away. They were driven through the roof of the neighbor woman's house. The candle-wicks fluttered and light came on them again. She saw the hound standing in the middle of the floor. She saw the corpse sitting where it had been laid and the eyes were now open.

"Fair Maid," said the voice of the Hunter-King,

"you have brought me back to life. I am a man under enchantment. There is a witch-woman in the wood that I gave my love to. She enchanted me so that the soul was out of my body, and wandering away. It was my soul you followed. And the enchantment was to be broken when I found a heart so faithful that it would follow my soul over the Quaking Bog, through the Burning Forest, and across the Icy Sea. You have brought my soul and my life back to me." Then she ran out of the neighbor's house.

The night after, in the Spae-Woman's house she finished weaving the threads that were on the loom. The next night she stitched the cloth and made the sixth shirt. The day after she went into the bog to gather the bog-down for the seventh shirt. She had gathered her basketful and was going through the wood about the hour of sunset. At the edge of the thin wood she saw the Hunter-King standing. He took her hands and his were warm hands. His brown face and his gentian-blue eyes were high and noble. And Sheen felt a joy like the sharpness of a sword when he sang to her about the brightness of her hair and the blue of her eyes. "O Maid," said he, "is there anything that binds you to this place?" Sheen showed him the bog-down in the basket and the woven thread that was round her neck. "Come with me to my kingdom," said he, "and you shall be my wife and the love of my heart." The next evening Sheen went with him. She took the six shirts she had spun and woven and stitched. The

Hunter-King lifted her before him on a black horse and they rode into his Kingdom.

And now Sheen was the wife of the Hunter-King. She would have been happy if her husband's sisters had been kind. But they were jealous and they made everything in the Castle unfriendly to her. And often they talked before her brother saying that Sheen was not noble at all, and that the reason she did not speak was because her language was a base one. They watched her when she went out to gather bog-down in the daytime, and they watched her when she spun by herself at night. Sheen longed for the days and nights to pass so that the last threads might be spun and woven and the last stitches put in the seventh shirt. Then her brothers would be with her. She could tell the King about herself and silence the bad talk of his sisters. But as she neared the end of her task she became more and more in dread.

The threads were spun and woven for the seventh shirt. The cloth was made and the first stitches were put in it. Then Sheen's little son was born. The King was away at the time, gathering his men together at far parts of the Kingdom, and he sent a message saying that Sheen and her baby were to be well-minded, and that his sisters were not to leave the chamber where she was until he returned.

On the third night, while Sheen was in her bed with her baby beside her, and while her sisters-in-law were in the room, a strange music was heard outside. It was played all round the King's house. Whoever heard it fell into deep slumber. The kern that were on guard slept. The maids that were whispering together fell into a slumber. And a deep sleep came upon Sheen and her child and on her three sisters-in-law who watched in the chamber.

Then a gray wolf that had been seen outside sprang in through the window opening. He took Sheen's child in his mouth. He sprang back through the window opening and was seen about the place no more.

Her sisters-in-law wakened while Sheen still slept. They went to tend it and found the child was gone. Then they were afraid of what their brother would do to them for letting this happen. They made a plot to clear themselves, and before Sheen wakened they had killed a little beast and smeared its blood upon the pillows of the bed.

When the King came into his wife's chamber he saw his sisters on the ground lamenting and tearing the hairs out of their heads. He went to where his wife was sleeping and saw blood upon her hands and upon the pillows. He turned on his sisters with his sword in his hand. They cried out that they could not have prevented the thing that had happened—that the Queen had laid hands on the child and having killed it had thrown its body to the gray wolf that had been watching outside.

And while they were speaking Sheen awakened. She put out her arms but her child was not beside her. She found blood upon the pillows. Then she heard her sisters-in-law accuse her to the King of having killed her child and flung its body to the gray wolf outside. She fell into a swoon and when she came out of it her mind was lost to her.

The King knelt to her and begged her to tell him what had happened. But she only knew she was to say no word. Then he used to watch her and he wondered why she cried no tear. On the fourth day after she rose from her bed, and searched the Castle for the piece of cloth she had spun and woven out of the bog-down. She found it and began to sew it for the seventh shirt. The King's sisters came to him and said, "The woman you brought here is of another race from ours. She has forgotten that a child was born to her, and that she killed it and flung its body to the gray wolf. She sits there now just stitching a garment." The King went and saw her stitching and stitching as if her life depended on each stitch she put into the cloth. He spoke to her and she looked up but did not speak. Then the King's heart was hardened. He took her and brought her outside the gate of the Castle. "Go back to the people you came from," said he, "for I cannot bear that you should be here, and not speak to me of what has happened." Sheen knew she was being sent from the house he had brought her to. A bitter cry came from her. Then the stitched cloth that was in her hand became bog-down and was blown away on the breeze. When she saw this happen she turned from the King's Castle and ran through the woods crying and crying.

She went through the woods for many days, living on berries and the water of springs. At last she came to the Spae-Woman's house. The Spae-Woman was before the door and she welcomed Sheen back. She gave her drinks she had made from strange herbs, and in a season Sheen's mind and health came back to her, and she knew all that had happened.

She thought she would win back her seven brothers, and then, with their help, win back her child and her husband. But she knew she would have to gather the bog-down, spin the threads and weave them all over again, as her tears and cries had broken her task. She told her story to the Spae-Woman. Then she went into silence again, gathering the bog-down and spinning the thread.

But when the first thread was spun the memory of her child blew against her heart and she cried tears down. The thread she had spun became bog-down and was blown away. For days she wept and wept. Then the Spae-Woman said to her, "Commit the child you have lost to Diachbha—that is, to Destiny—and Diachbha may bring it about that he shall be the one that will restore your seven brothers their human forms. And when you have committed your lost little son to Diachbha go back to your husband and tell him all you have lived through."

Sheen, believing in the Spae-Woman's wisdom, did what was told her. She made an image of her lost little son with leaves and left it on the top of the house where it was blown away by the winds. Then she was ready to go back to her husband and tell him all that had happened in her life. But on the day she was bringing the last pitcher of water from the well she met him on the path before her. "Do you remember that I carried you across the bog?" he said. "And do you remember that I followed your soul?" said she. These were the first words she ever spoke to him.

They went back together to the Spae-Woman's and she told him all that had been in her life. He told her how his sisters had acknowledged that they had spoken falsely against her.

He took her back to his own Kingdom, and there, as King and Queen they still live. But the name she bears is not Sheen or Storm now. Two sons more were born to her. But her seven brothers are still seven wild geese, and the Queen has found no trace of her first-born son. But the Spae-Woman has had a dream, and the dream has revealed this to her: the Son that Sheen lost is in the world, and if the maiden who will come to love him, will give seven drops of her heart's blood, the Queen's seven brothers will regain their human forms.

"So that is the Unique Tale," said the Old Woman of Beare. "If you ever find out what went before it and what comes after it come back here and tell it to me. But I don't think you'll get the rest of it," said she, "seeing that the two of you weren't able to count the horns outside." She went on talking and talking, Gilly and the King's Son hearing what she said when she spoke in a sudden high voice, and not hearing when she murmured on as if talking to the ashes or to the pot or to the corncrake, the cuckoo or the swallow that were picking grains off the floor. "If you see Laheen the Eagle again, or Blackfoot the Elk or the Crow of Achill tell them to come and visit me sometime. I'm all alone here except for my swallow and cuckoo and corncrake. And mind you, great Kings and Princes used to come to see me." So she went on talking in low tones and in sudden high tones.

"You must come with me and help me to get the rest of the Unique Tale," said the King of Ireland's Son.

"That I'll do," said Gilly of the Goatskin. "But I must get a name first. Old Mother," said he, to the Old Woman of Beare. "You must now give me a name."

"I'll give you a name," said the Old Woman of Beare, "but you must stand before me and strip off the goatskin that covers you."

Gilly pulled at the strings and the goatskin fell on the ground. The Old Woman of Beare nodded her head. "You have the stars on your breast that denote the Son of a King," she said.

"The Son of a King—me!" said Gilly of the Goatskin.

"You have the stars on your breast," said the Old Woman of Beare.

Gilly looked at himself and saw the three stars on his breast. "If I am the Son of a King I never knew it until now," he said.

"You are the Son of a King," said the Old Woman of Beare, "and I will give you a name when you come back to me. But I want you, first of all, to find out what happened to the Crystal Egg."

"The Crystal Egg!" said Gilly in great surprise.

"The Crystal Egg indeed," said the Old Woman of Beare. "You must know that it was stolen out of the nest of Laheen the Eagle, and the creature that stole it was the Crow of Achill. But what happened to the Crystal Egg after that no one knows."

"I myself had it after that," said Gilly, "and it was stolen from me by Rory the Fox. And then it was put under a goose to hatch."

"A goose to hatch the Crystal Egg after an Eagle had half-hatched it! Aye, aye, to be sure, that's right," said the Old Woman of Beare. "And now you must go and find out what happened to it. Go now, and when you come back I will give you your name."

"I will do that," said Gilly of the Goatskin. Then he turned to the King's Son. "Three days before Midsummer's Day meet me on the road to the Town of the Red Castle, and I will go with you to find out what went before and what comes after the Unique Tale," he said.

"I will meet you," said the King of Ireland's Son.

The two youths went to the table and ate slices of the unwasted loaf and drank draughts from the inexhaustible bottle. "I shall stay here to practice sword cuts and sword thrusts," said the King's Son, "until four days before Midsummer's Day." The two youths went to the door.

"Seven waves of goodluck to you, Old Woman of Beare," said Gilly of the Goatskin.

"May your double be slain and yourself remain," said the King's Son.

Then they went out together, but not along the same path did the two youths go.

XV

GILLY slept as he traveled that night, for he fell in with a man who was driving a load of hay to the fair, and when he got into the cart he lay against the hay and slept. When he parted with the carter he cut a holly stick and journeyed along the road by himself. At the fall of night he came to a place that made him think he had been there before: he looked around and then he knew that this was the place he had lived in when he had the Crystal Egg. He looked to see if the house was there: it was, and people were living in it, for he saw smoke coming out of the chimney. It was dark now and Gilly thought he could not do better than take shelter in that house.

He went to the door and knocked. There was a lot of rattling behind, and then a crooked old woman opened the door to him. "What do you want?" said she.

"Can I have shelter here for tonight, ma'am?" said Gilly.

"You can get no shelter here," said the old woman, "and I'd advise you to begone."

"May I ask who lives here?" said Gilly, putting his foot inside the door.

"Six very honest men whose business keeps them out until two and three in the morning," said the crooked old woman.

Gilly guessed that the honest men whose business kept them out until two and three in the morning were the robbers he had heard about. And he thought they might be the very men who had carried off the Spae-Woman's goose and the Crystal Egg along with it. "Would you tell me, good woman," said Gilly, "did your six honest men ever bring to this house an old hatching goose?"

"They did indeed," said the crooked woman, "and a heart-scald the same old hatching goose is. It goes round the house and round the house, trying to hatch the cups I leave out of my hands."

Then Gilly pushed the door open wide and stepped into the house.

"Don't stay in the house," said the crooked old woman. "I'll tell you the truth now. My masters are robbers, and they'll skin you alive if they find you here when they come back in the morning."

"It's more likely I'll skin them alive," said Gilly, and he looked so fierce that he fairly frightened the old

. 151 .

woman. "And if you don't satisfy me with supper and a bed I'll leave you to meet them hanging from the door."

The crooked old woman was so terrified that she gave him a supper of porridge and showed him a bed to sleep in. He turned in and slept. He was roused by a candle being held to his eyes. He wakened up and saw six robbers standing round him with knives in their hands.

"What brings you under our roof?" said the Captain. "Answer me now before we skin you as we would skin an eel."

"Speak up and answer the Captain," said the robbers.

"Why shouldn't I be under this roof?" said Gilly. "I am the Master-Thief of the World."

The robbers put their hands on their knees and laughed at that. Gilly jumped out of the bed. "I have come to show you the arts of thievery and roguery," said he. "I'll show you some tricks that will let you hold up your heads amongst the thieves and robbers of the world."

He looked so bold and he spoke so bold that the robbers began to think he might have some reason for talking as he did. They left him and went off to their beds. Gilly slept again. At the broad noon they were all sitting at breakfast—Gilly and the six robbers. A farmer went past leading a goat to the fair.

"Could any of you steal that goat without doing any violence to the man who is driving it?" said Gilly.

"I couldn't," said one robber, and "I couldn't," said another robber, and "I'd be hardly able to do that myself," said the Captain of the Robbers.

"I can do it," said Gilly. "I'll be back with the goat before you are through with your breakfast." He went outside.

Gilly knew that country well and he ran through the wood until he was a bend of the road ahead of the farmer who was leading his goat to the fair. He took off one shoe and left it in the middle of the road. He ran on then until he was round another bend of the road. He took off the other shoe and left it down. Then he hid behind the hedge and waited.

The farmer came to where the first shoe was. "That's not a bad shoe," said he, "and if there was a comrade for it, it would be worth picking up." He went on then and came to where the other shoe was lying. "Here is the comrade," said he, "and it's worth my while now to go back for the first." He tied the goat to the milestone and went back.

As soon as the farmer had turned his back, Gilly took the collar off the goat, left it on the milestone and took the goat through a gap in the hedge. He brought it to the house before the robbers were through with their breakfast. They were all terribly surprised. The Captain began to bite at his nails.

The farmer, with the two shoes under his arm, came to where he had left the goat. The goat was gone and its collar was left on the milestone. He knew that a robber had taken his goat. "And I had promised Ann, my wife, to buy her a new shawl at the fair," said he. "She'll never stop scolding me if I go back to her now with one hand as long as the other. The best thing I can do is to take a sheep out of my field and sell that. Then when she is in good humor on account of getting the shawl I'll tell her about the loss of my goat." So the farmer went back to the field.

They were sitting down to a game of cards after breakfast—the six robbers and Gilly—when they saw the farmer going past with the sheep. "I'll be bound that he'll watch that sheep more closely than he watched the goat," said one of the robbers. "Could any of you steal that sheep without doing him any violence?" said Gilly. "I couldn't," said one robber, and "I couldn't," said another robber. "I could hardly do that myself," said the Captain of the Robbers. "I'll bring the sheep here before you're through with the game of cards," said Gilly.

The farmer was just past the milestone when he saw a man hanging on a tree. "The saints between us and harm," said he, "do they hang men along this road?" Now the man hanging from the tree was Gilly. He had fastened himself to a branch with his belt, putting it under his armpits. He slipped down from the branch and ran till he was ahead of the farmer. The farmer saw another man hanging from a tree. "The saints preserve us," said he, "sure, it's not possible that they hanged two men along this road?" Gilly slipped down from that tree too and ran on until he was ahead of the farmer again. The farmer saw a third man hanging from a tree. "Am I leaving my senses?" said he. "I'll go back and see if the other men are hanging there as I thought they were." He tied the sheep to a bush and went back. As soon as he turned, Gilly slipped down from the tree, took the sheep through a gap, and got back to the robbers before they were through with the game. All the robbers said it was a wonderful thing he had done. The Captain of the Robbers was left standing by himself scratching his head.

The farmer found no men hanging on trees and he thought he was out of his mind. He came back and he found his sheep gone. "What will I do now?" said he. "I daren't let Ann know I lost a goat and a sheep until I put her into good humor by showing the shawl I bought her at the fair. There's nothing to be done now, but take a bullock out of the field and sell it at the fair." He went to the field then, took a bullock out of it, and passed the house just as the robbers were lighting their pipes. "If he watched the goat and the sheep closely he'll watch the bullock nine times as closely," said one of the robbers.

"Which of you could take the bullock without doing the man any violence?" said Gilly. "I couldn't," said one robber, and "I couldn't," said another robber. "If you could do it," said the Captain of the Robbers to Gilly, "I'll resign my command and give it to you."

· 155 ·

"Done," said Gilly, and he went out of the house again.

He went quickly through the wood, and when he came near where the farmer was he began to bleat like a goat. The farmer stopped and listened. Then Gilly began to baa like the sheep. "That sounds very like my goat and sheep," said the farmer. "Maybe they weren't taken at all, but just strayed off. If I can get them now, I needn't make any excuses to Ann, my wife." He tied the bullock to a tree and went into the wood. As soon as he did, Gilly slipped out, took the bullock by the rope and hurried back to the house. The robbers were gathered at the door to watch for his coming back. When they saw him with the bullock they threw up their hats. "This man must be our Captain," they said. The Captain was biting his lips and his nails. At last he took off his hat with the feathers in it and gave it to Gilly. "You're our Captain now," said the robbers.

Gilly ordered that the goat, the sheep, and the bullock be put into the byre, that the door he locked and the key be given to him. All that was done. Then said he to all the robbers, "I demand to know what became of the Crystal Egg that was with the goose you stole from the Spae-Woman." "The Crystal Egg," said one of the robbers. "It hatched, and a queer bird came out of it." "Where is that bird now?" said Gilly. "On the waves of the lake near at hand," said the robbers. "We see it every day." "Take me to the lake till I see the Bird out of the Crystal Egg," said Gilly. They locked the door of the house behind them, and the seven, Gilly at their head, wearing the hat with feathers, marched down to the lake.

XVI

THEN they showed him the bird that was on the waves of the lake—a swan she was and she floated proudly. The swan came toward them and as she drew nearer they could hear her voice. The sounds she made were not like any sound of birds, but like the sounds bards make chanting their verses. Words came on high notes and low notes, but they were like words in a strange language. And still the swan chanted as she drew near to the shore where Gilly and the six robbers stood.

She spread out her wings, and, raising her neck she curved it, while she stayed watching the men on the bank. "Hear the Swan of Endless Tales—the Swan of Endless Tales" she sang in words they knew. Then she raised herself out of the water, turned round in the air, and flew back to the middle of the lake.

"Time for us to be leaving the place when there is a bird on the lake that can speak like that," said Mogue, who had been the Captain of the Robbers. "Tonight I'm leaving this townland."

"And I am leaving too," said another robber. "And I too," said another. "And I may be going away from this place," said Gilly of the Goatskin.

The robbers went away from him and back to the house and Gilly sat by the edge of the lake waiting to see if the Swan of Endless Tales would come back and tell him something. She did not come. As Gilly sat there the farmer who had lost his goat, his sheep, and his bullock came by. He was dragging one foot after the other and looking very downcast. "What is the matter with you, honest man?" said Gilly.

The farmer told him how he had lost his goat, his sheep, and his bullock. He told him how he had thought he heard his goat bleating and his sheep ba'ing, and how he went through the wood to search for them, and how his bullock was gone when he came back to the road. "And what to say to my wife Ann I don't know," said he, "particularly as I have brought no shawl to put her in good humor. Heavy is the blame she'll give me on account of my losing a goat, a sheep, and a bullock."

Gilly took a key out of his pocket. "Do you see this key?" said he. "Take it and open the byre door at such a place, and you'll find in that byre your goat, your sheep, and your bullock. There are robbers in that house, but if they try to prevent your taking your own tell them that all the threshers of the country are coming to beat them with flails." The farmer took the key and went away very thankful to Gilly. The story says that he got back his goat, his sheep, and his bullock and made it an excuse that he had seen three magpies on the road for not going to the fair to buy a shawl for his wife Ann. The robbers were very frightened when he told them about the threshers coming and they went away from that part of the country.

As for Gilly, he thought he would go back to the Old Woman of Beare for his name. He took the path by the edge of the lake. And as he journeyed along with his holly-stick in his hand he heard the Swan of Endless Tales chanting.

THE TOWN OF THE RED CASTLE

I

FLANN was the name that the Old Woman of Beare gave to Gilly of the Goatskin when he came back to tell her that the Swan of Endless Tales had been hatched out of the Crystal Egg. He went from her house then and came to where the King of Ireland's Son waited for him. The two comrades went along a well-traveled road. As they went on they fell in with men driving herds of ponies, men carrying packs on their backs, men with tools for working gold and silver, bronze and iron. Every man whom they asked said, "We are going to the Town of the Red Castle, and to the great fair that will be held there." The King's Son and Flann thought they should go to the Town of the Red Castle too, for where so many people would be, there was a chance of hearing what went before and what came after the Unique Tale. So they went on.

And when they had come to a well that was under a great rock those whom they were with halted. They said it was the custom for the merchants and sellers to wait there for a day and to go into the Town of the Red Castle the day following. "On this day," they said, "the people of the Town celebrate the Festival of Midsummer, and they do not like a great company of people to go into their Town until the Festival is over."

The King of Ireland's Son and Flann went on, and they were let into the town. The people had lighted great fires in their marketplace and they were driving their cattle through the fires: "If there be evil on you, may it burn, may it burn," they were crying. They were afraid that witches and enchanters might come into the town with the merchants and the sellers, and that was the reason they did not permit a great company to enter.

The fires in all their houses had been quenched that day, and they might not be lighted except from the fires the cattle had gone through. The fires were left blazing high and the King's Son and Flann spent hours watching them, and watching the crowds that were around.

Then the time came to take fire to the houses. They who came for fire were all young maidens. Each came into the light of one of the great fires, took coals from a fire that had burnt low, placed them in a new earthen vessel and went away. Flann thought that all the maidens were beautiful and wonderful, although the King's Son told him that some were black-faced, and some crop-headed, and some hunchbacked. Then a maiden came, who was so high above the rest that Flann had no words to speak of her.

She had silver on her head and silver on her arms, and the people around the fires all bowed to her. She had black, black hair and she had a smiling face—not hap-

Then a maiden came.

pily smiling, but proudly smiling. Flann thought that a star had bent down with her. And when she had taken the fire and had gone away, Flann said, "She is surely the King's daughter!"

"She is," said the King of Ireland's Son. "The people here have spoken her name." "What is her name?" asked Flann. "It is Lassarina," said the King's Son, "Flame-of-Wine."

"Shall we see her again?" said Flann.

"That I do not know," said the King's Son. "Come now, and let us ask the people here if they have knowledge of the Unique Tale."

"Wait," said Flann, "they are talking about Princess Flame-of-Wine." He did not move, but listened to what was said. All said that the King's daughter was proud. Some said she was beautiful, but others answered that her lips were thin, and her eyes were mocking. No other maidens came for fire. Flann stood before the one that still blazed, and thought and thought. The King's Son asked many if they had knowledge of the Unique Tale, but no one had heard of it. Some told him that there would be mechants and sellers from many parts of the world at the fair that would be held on the morrow, and that there would be a chance of meeting one who had knowledge of it. Then the King's Son went with one who brought him to a Brufir's—that is, to a House of Hospitality maintained by the King for strangers. As for Flann, he sat looking into the fire until it died down, and then he slept before it.

II

FLANN was wakened by a gander and his flock of geese that stood round him, shook their wings and set up their goose-gabble. It was day then, although there was still a star in the sky. He threw furze-roots where there was a glow, and made a fire blaze up again. Then the dogs of the town came down to look at him, and then stole away.

Horns were blown outside, and the watchman opened the gates. Flann shook himself and stood up to see the folk that were coming in. First came the men who drove the mountain ponies that had lately fed with the deer in wild places. Then came men in leathern jerkins who led wide-horned bulls—a black bull and a white bull, and a white bull and a black bull, one after the other. Then there were men who brought in high, swift hounds, three to each leash they held. Women in brown cloaks carried cages of birds. Men carried on their shoulders and in their belts tools for working gold and silver, bronze and iron. And there were calves and sheep, and great horses and weighty chariots, and colored cloths, and things closed in packs that merchants carried on their shoulders. The famous bards, and storytellers, and harpists would not come until noontime when the business of the fair would have abated, but with the crowd of beggars came ballad-singers, and the tellers of the stories that were called "Go-by-the-Market-Stake," because they were told around the stake in the market place and were very common.

And at the tail of the comers whom did Flann see but Mogue, the Captain of the Robbers!

Mogue wore a hare-skin cap, his left eye protruded as usual, and he walked limpingly. He had a pack on his back, and he led a small, swift looking horse of a reddish color. Flann called to him as he passed and Mogue gave a great start. He grinned when he saw it was Flann and walked up to him.

"Mogue," said Flann, "what are you doing in the Town of the Red Castle?"

"I'm here to sell a few things," said Mogue, "this little horse," said he, "and a few things I have in my pack."

"And where are your friends?" asked Flann.

"My band, do you mean?" said Mogue. "Sure, they all left me when you proved you were the better robber. What are you doing here?"

"I have no business at all," said Flann.

"By the Hazel! that's what I like to hear you say. Join me then. You and me would do well together."

"I won't join you," said Flann.

"I'd rather have you with me than the whole of the band. What were they anyway? Cabbageheads!"

Mogue winked with his protruding eye. "Wait till you see me again," said he. "I've the grandest things in my pack." He went on leading the little horse. Then Flann set out to look for the King's Son.

He found him at the door of the Brufir's, and they drank bowls of milk and ate oaten bread together, and then went to the gate of the town to watch the notable people who were coming in.

And with the bards and harpers and Kings' envoys who came in, the King's Son saw his two half-brothers, Dermott and Downal. He hailed them and they knew him and came up to him gladly.. The King's Son made Flann known to them, saying that he too was the son of a King.

They looked fine youths, Downal and Dermott, in their red cloaks, with their heads held high, and a brag in their walk and their words. They left their horses with the grooms and walked with Flann and the King's Son. They were tall and ruddy; the King's Son was more brown in the hair and more hawklike in the face: the three were different from the dark-haired, dark-eyed, red-lipped lad to whom the Old Woman of Beare had given the name of Flann.

No one had seen the King who lived in the Red Castle, Dermott and Downal told the other two. He was called the Wry-faced King, and, on account of his disfigurement, he let no one but his Councillors see him.

"We are to go to his Castle today," said Dermott and Downal. "You come too, brother," said he to the King's Son.

"And you too, comrade," said Downal to Flann.

"Why should we not all go? By Ogma! Are we not all sons of Kings?"

Flann wondered if he would see the King's daughter, Flame-of-Wine. He would surely go to the Castle.

They drank ale, played chess, and talked until it was afternoon. Then the grooms who were with Downal and Dermott brought the four youths new red cloaks. They put them on and went toward the King's Castle.

"Brother," said Dermott to the King's Son, "I want to tell you that we are not going back to our father's Castle nor to his Kingdom. We have taken the world for our pillow. We are going to leave the grooms asleep one fine morning, and go as the salmon goes down the river."

"Why do you want to leave our father's Kingdom?"

"Because we don't want to rule nor to learn to rule. We'll let you, brother, do all that. We're going to learn the trade of a swordsmith. We would make fine swords. And with the King of Senlabor there is a famous swordsmith, and we are going to learn the trade from him."

The four went to the Red Castle, and they were brought in and they went and sat on the benches to wait for the King's Steward who would receive them. And while they waited they watched the play of a pet fox in the courtyard. Flann was wondering all the time if the Princess Flame-of-Wine would pass through the courtyard or come into the hall where they waited.

Then he saw her come up the courtyard. She saw the

youths in the hall and she turned round to watch the pet fox for a while. Then she came into the chamber and stood near the door.

She wore a mask across her face, but her brow and mouth and chin were shown. The youths saluted her, and she bent her head to them. One of the women who had brought birds to the Fair followed her, bringing a cage. Flame-of-Wine talked to this woman in a strange language.

Although she talked to the woman, Flann saw that she watched his three companions. Him she did not notice, because the bench on which he sat was behind the others. Flame-of-Wine looked at the King's Son first, and then turned her eyes from him. She bent her head to listen to what Downal and Dermott were saying. Flann she did not look at at all, and he became sick at heart of the Red Castle.

The King's Steward came into the Hall and when he announced who the youths were—three sons of the King of Ireland traveling with their foster brother—Flame-of-Wine went over and spoke to them. "May we see you tomorrow, Kings' Sons," she said. "Tomorrow is our feast of the Gathering of Apples. It might be pleasant for you to hear music in the King's garden." She smiled on Downal and Dermott and on the King's Son and went out of the Chamber.

The King's Steward feasted the four youths and afterwards made them presents. But Flann did not heed what he ate nor what he heard said, nor what present was given him.

III

THE four youths left the Castle and Downal and Dermott took their own way when they came to the footbridge that was across the river. Then when they were crossing it the King's Son and Flann saw two figures—a middle-aged, sturdy man and an old, broken-looking woman—meet before the Bull's Field. "It is the Gobaun Saor," said the King's Son. "It is the Spae-Woman," said Flann. They went to them, each wishing to greet his friend and helper.

There they saw a sturdy, middle-aged man and a broken-looking old woman. But the woman looking on the man saw one who had full wisdom to plan and full strength to build, whose wisdom and whose strength could neither grow nor diminish. And the man looking on the woman saw one whose brow had all quiet, whose heart had all benignity. "Hail, Gobaun, Builder for the Gods," said the woman. "Hail, Grania Oi, Reconciler for the Gods," said the man.

Then the two youths came swiftly up to them, and the King's Son greeted the middle-aged man, and Flann kissed the hands of the old woman.

"What of your search, King's Son?" said the Gobaun Saor.

"I have found the Unique Tale, but not what went before nor what comes after it," said the King's Son.

"I will clear the Sword of Light of its stain when you

bring me the whole of the Unique Tale," said the Gobaun Saor.

"I would search the whole world for it," said the King's
Son. "But now the time is becoming short for me."

"Be quick and active," said the Gobaun Saor. "I
have set up my forge," said he, "outside the town between two high stones. When you bring the whole of
the Tale to me I shall clear your sword."

"Will you not tell him, Gobaun Saor," said the Spae-
Woman, "where he may find the one who will tell him
the rest of the story?"

"If he sees one he knows in this town," said the Gobaun Saor, "let him mount a horse he has mounted
before and pursue that one and force him to tell what
went before and what comes after the Unique Tale."

Saying this the Gobaun Saor turned away and walked
along the road that went out of the town.

The Spae-Woman had brought besoms to the town
to sell. She showed the two youths the little house she
lived in while she was there. It was filled with the
heather-stalks which she bound together for besoms.

They left the Spae-Woman and went through the
town, the King of Ireland's Son searcing every place
for a man he knew or a horse he had mounted before,
while Flann thought about the Princess Flame-of-Wine,
and how little she considered him beside the King's Son
and Dermott and Downal. They came to where a crowd
was standing before a conjurer's booth. They halted and
stood waiting for the conjurer to appear. He came out

and put a ladder standing upright with nothing to lean
against and began climbing up. Up, up, up, he went,
and the ladder grew higher and higher as he climbed.
Flann though he would climb into the sky. Then the
ladder got smaller and smaller and Flann saw the conjurer coming down on the other side. "He has come
here to take that horse," said a voice behind the King
of Ireland's Son.

The King's Son looked round, and on the outskirts of
the crowd he saw a man with a hareskin cap and a protruding eye who was holding a reddish horse, while
he watched the conjuror. The King of Ireland's Son
knew the horse—it was the Slight Red Steed that had
carried him and Fedelma from the Enchanter's house
and had brought him to the Cave where he had found
the Sword of Light. He looked at the conjuror again
and he saw he was no other than the Enchanter of the
Black Back-Lands. Then it crossed his mind what the
Gobaun Saor had said to him.

He had seen a man he knew and a horse he had
mounted before. He was to mount that horse, follow
the man, and force him to tell the rest of the Unique
Tale.

The King's Son drew back to the outskirts of the
crowd. He snatched the bridle from the hands of Mogue,
the man who held it, and jumped up on the back of the
Slight Red Steed.

As soon as he did this the ladder that was standing
upright fell on the ground. The people shouted and

broke away. And then the King's Son saw the Enchanter jump across a house and make for the gate of the town.

But if he could jump across a house so could the Slight Red Steed. The King's Son turned its head, plucked at its rein, and over the same house it sprang too. The more he ran the more swift the Enchanter became. He jumped over the gate of the town, the Slight Red Steed after him. He went swiftly across the country, making high springs over ditches and hedges. No other steed but the Slight Red Steed could have kept its rider in sight of him.

IV

UP hill and down dale the Enchanter went, but, mounted on the Slight Red Steed, the King of Ireland's Son was in hot pursuit. The Enchanter raced up the side of the seventh hill, and when the King's Son came to the top of it he found no one in sight.

He raced on, however, and he passed a dead man hanging from a tree. He raced on and on, but still the Enchanter was not to be seen. Then the thought came into his mind that the man who was hanging from the tree and who he thought was dead was the crafty old Enchanter. He turned the Slight Red Steed round and raced back. The man that had been hanging from the tree was there no longer.

The King's Son turned his horse amongst the trees and began to search for the Enchanter. He found no

trace of him. "I have lost again," he said. Then he threw
the bridle on the neck of the horse and he said, "Go
your own way now, my Slight Red Steed."

When he said that the Slight Red Steed twitched its
ears and galloped toward the West. It went through
woods and across streams, and when the crows were
flying home and the kites were flying abroad it brought
the King's Son to a stone house standing in the middle
of a bog. "It may be the Enchanter is in this house,"
said the King's Son. He jumped off the Slight Red
Steed, pushed the door of the house open, and there,
seated on a chair in the middle of the floor with a woman
sitting beside him, was the Enchanter of the Black Back-
Lands. "So," said the Enchanter, "my Slight Red Steed
has brought you to me."

"So," said the King's Son, "I have found you, my
crafty old Enchanter."

"And now that you have found me, what do you want
of me?" said the Enchanter.

"Your head," said the King's Son, drawing the tarnished Sword of Light.

"Will nothing less than my head content you?" said
the Enchanter.

"Nothing less—unless it be what went before, and
what comes after the Unique Tale."

"The Unique Tale," said the Enchanter. "I will tell
you what I know of it." Thereupon he began—

I was a Druid and the Son of a Druid, and I had
learned the language of the birds. And one morning, as

I walked abroad, I heard a blackbird and a robin talking, and when I heard what they said I smiled to myself.

"Now the woman I had just married noticed that I kept smiling, and she questioned me. 'Why do you keep smiling to yourself?' I would not tell her. 'Is that not the truth?' " said the Enchanter to a woman who sat beside him. "It is the truth," said she.

"On the third day I was still smiling to myself, and my wife questioned me, and when I did not answer threw dishwater into my face. 'May blindness come upon you if you do not tell me why you are smiling,' said she. Then I told her why I smiled to myself. I had heard what the birds said. The blackbird said to the robin, 'Do you know that just under where we are sitting are three rods of enchantment, and if one were to take one of them and strike a man with it, he would be changed to any creature one named?' That is what I had heard the birds say and I smiled because I was the only creature who knew about the rods of enchantment.

"My wife made me show her where the rods were. She cut one of them when I went away. That evening she came behind me and struck me with a rod. 'Go out now and roam as a wolf,' she said, and there and then I was changed into a wolf. 'Is that not true?' " said he to the woman. "It is true," she said.

"And being changed into a wolf, I went through the woods seeking wolf's meat. And now you must ask my wife to tell you more of the story."

The King of Ireland's Son turned to the woman who

sat on the seat next the Enchanter, and asked her to tell him more of the story. And thereupon she began—

Before all that happened I was known as the Maid of the Green Mantle. One day a King rode up a mountain with five score followers and a mist came on them as they rode. The King saw his followers no more. He called out after a while and four score answered him. And he called out again after another while and two score answered him. And after another while he called out again and only a score answered him through the mist, and when he called out again no one answered him at all.

"The King went up the mountain until he came to the place where I lived with the Druids who reared me. He stayed long in that place. The King loved me for a while and I loved the King, and when he went away I followed him.

"Because he would not come back to me I enchanted him so that there were times when he was left between life and death. Once when he was seemingly dead a girl watched by him, and she followed his spirit into many terrible places and so broke my enchantment."

"Sheen was the girl's name," said the King of Ireland's Son.

"Sheen was her name," said the woman. "He brought her to his Kingdom, and made her his queen. After that I married the man who is here now—the Enchanter of the Black Back-Lands, the Son of the Druid of the

Gray Rock. Ask him now to tell you the rest of the story."

"When she changed me into a gray wolf," said the Enchanter, "I went through the woods searching for what a wolf might eat, but could find nothing to stay my hunger. Then I came back and stood outside my house and the woman who had been called the Maid of the Green Mantle came to me. 'I will give you back your human form,' she said, 'if you do as I bid you.'

"I promised her I would do as she bade.

"She bade me go to a King's house where a child had been born. She bade me steal the child away. I went to the King's house. I went into the chamber and I stole the child from the mother's side. Then I ran through the woods. But in the end I fell into a trap that the Giant Crom Duv had set for the wolves that chased his stray cattle.

"For a night I lay in the trap with the child beside me. Then Crom Duv came and lifted out wolf and child. Three Hags with Long Teeth were there when he took us out of the trap, and he gave the child to one of them, telling her to rear it so that the child might be a servant for him.

"He put me into a sack, promising himself that he would give me a good beating. He left me on the floor of his house. But while he was gone for his club I bit my way out of the sack and made my escape. I came back to my own house, and my wife struck me with the wand of enchantment, and changed me from a wolf into a man again. 'Is that not true?' " said he to the woman.

"It is true," said she.

"That is all of the Unique Tale that I know," said the Enchanter of the Black Back-Lands, "and now that I have told it to you, put up your sword."

"I will put up no sword," said the King of Ireland's Son, "until you tell me what King and Queen were the father and mother of the child that was reared by the Hags of the Long Teeth."

"I made no promise to tell you that," said the Enchanter of the Black Back-Lands. "You have got the story you asked for, and now let me see your back going through my door."

"Yes, you have got the story, and be off with you now," said the woman who sat by the fire.

He put up his sword; he went to the door; he left the house of the Enchanter of the Black Back-Lands. He mounted the Slight Red Steed and rode off. He knew now what went before and what came after the Unique Tale. The Gobaun Saor would clean the blemish of the blade of the Sword of Light and would show him how to come to the Land of Mist. Then he would win back his love Fedelma.

He thought too on the tidings he had for his comrade Flann—Flann was the Son of the King who was called the Hunter-King and of Sheen whose brothers had been changed into seven wild geese. He shook his

horse's reins and went back toward the Town of the
Red Castle.

V

FLANN thought upon the Princess Flame-of-Wine. He
walked through the town after the King's Son had
ridden after the Enchanter, without noticing anyone
until he heard a call and saw Mogue standing beside a
little tent that he had set up before the Bull's Field.

Flann went to Mogue and found him very disconsolate on account of the loss of the horse he had brought
into the town. "This is a bad town to be in," said Mogue,
"and unless I persuade yourself to become partners with
me I shall have done badly in it. Join with me now and
we'll do some fine feats together."

"It would not become a King's Son to join with a rob-
ber-captain," said Flann.

"Fine talk, fine talk," said Mogue. He thought that
Flann was jesting with him when he spoke of himself
as a King's Son.

"I want to sell three treasures I have with me," said
Mogue. "I have the most wonderful things that were
ever brought into this town."

"Show them to me," said Flann.

Mogue opened one of his packs and took out a box.
When he opened this box a fragrance came such as Flann
had never felt before. "What is that that smells like a
garden of sweet flowers?" said Flann.

"It is the Rose of Sweet Smells," said Mogue, and he took a little rose out of the box. "It never withers and its fragrance is never any less. It is a treasure for a King's daughter. But I will not show it in this town."

"And what is that shining thing in the box?"

"It is the Comb of Magnificence. That is another treasure for a King's daughter. The maiden who would wear it would look the most queenly woman in the Kingdom. But I won't show that either."

"What else have you, Mogue?"

"A girdle. The woman who wears it would have to speak the truth."

Flann thought he would do much to get the Rose of Sweet Smells or the Comb of Magnificence and bring them as presents to the Princess Flame-of-Wine.

He slept in Mogue's tent, and at the peep of day, he rose up and went to the House of Hospitality where Dermott and Downal were. With them he would go to the King's orchard, and he would see, and perhaps he would speak to, Flame-of-Wine. But Dermott and Downal were not in the Brufir's. Flann wakened their grooms and he and they made search for the two youths. But there was no trace of Dermott and Downal. It seemed they had left before daybreak with their horses. Flann went with the grooms to the gate of the town. There they heard from the watchman that the two youths had gone through the gate and that they had told the watchman to tell the grooms that they had gone to take the world for their pillow.

The grooms were dismayed to hear this, and so indeed was Flann. Without the King's Son and without Downal and Dermott how would he go to the King's Garden? He went back to Mogue's tent to consider what he should do. And first he thought he would not go to the Festival of the Gathering of the Apples, as he knew that Flame-of-Wine had only asked him with his comrades. And then he thought that whatever else happened he would go to the King's orchard and see Flame-of-Wine.

If he had one of the wonderful things that Mogue had shown him—the Rose of Sweet Smells or the Comb of Magnificence! These would show her that he was of some consequence. If he had either of these wonderful things and offered it to her she might be pleased with him!

He sat outside the tent and waited for Mogue to return. When he came Flann said to him, "I will go with you as a servant, and I will serve you well although I am a King's Son, if you will give me something now."

"What do you want from me?" said Mogue.

"Give me the Rose of Sweet Smells," said Flann.

"Sure that's the finest thing I have. I couldn't give you that."

"I will serve you for two years if you will give it to me," said Flann.

"No," said Mogue.

"I will serve you for three years if you will give it to me," said Flann.

"I will give it to you if you will serve me for three years." Thereupon Mogue opened his pack and took the box out. He opened it and put the Rose of Sweet Smells into Flann's hand.

At once Flann started off for the King's orchard. The Steward who had seen him the day before signed to the servants to let him pass through the gate. He went into the King's orchard.

Maidens were singing the "Song for the Time of the Blossoming of the Apple trees" and all that day and night Flann held their song in his mind—

> The touch of hands that drew it down
> Kindled to blossom all the bough—
> O breathe the wonder of the branch,
> And let it through the darkness go!

Youths were gathering apples, and the Princess Flame-of-Wine walked by herself on the orchard paths.

At last she came to where Flann stood and lifting her eyes she looked at him. "I had companions," said Flann, "but they have gone away."

"They are unmannerly," said Flame-of-Wine with anger, and she turned away.

Flann took the rose from under his cloak. Its fragrance came to Flame-of-Wine and she turned to him again.

"This is the Rose of Sweet Smells," said Flann. "Will you take it from me, Princess?"

She came back to him and took the rose in her hand, and there was wonder in her face.

"It will never wither, and its fragrance will never fail," said Flann. "It is the Rose of Sweet Smells. A King's daughter should have it."

Flame-of-Wine held the rose in her hand, and smiled on Flann. "What is your name, King's Son?" said she, with bright and friendly eyes.

"Flann," he said.

"Walk with me, Flann," said she. They walked along the orchard paths, and the youths and maidens turned toward the fragrance that the Rose of Sweet Smells gave. Flame-of-Wine laughed, and said, "They all wonder at the treasure you have brought me, Flann. If you could hear what I shall tell them about you! I shall tell them that you are the son of a King of Arabia—no less. They will believe me because you have brought me such a treasure! I suppose there is nothing more wonderful than this rose!"

Then Flann told her about the other wonderful thing he had seen—the Comb of Magnificence. "A King's daughter should have such a treasure," said Flame-of-Wine. "Oh, how jealous I should be if someone brought the Comb of Magnificence to either of my two sisters— to Bloom-of-Youth or Breast-of-Light. I should think then that this rose was not such a treasure after all."

When he was leaving the orchard she plucked a flower and gave it to him. "Come and walk in the orchard with me to-morrow," she said.

"Surely I will come," said Flann.

"Bring the Comb of Magnificence to me too," said

she. "I could not be proud of this rose, and I could not love you so well for bringing it to me if I thought that any other maiden had the Comb of Magnificence. Bring it to me, Flann."

"I will bring it to you," said Flann.

VI

HE was at the gate of the town when the King of Ireland's Son rode back on the Slight Red Steed. The King's Son dismounted, put his arm about Flann and told him that he now had the whole of the Unique Tale. They sat before Mogue's tent, and the King's Son told Flann the whole of the story he had searched for—how a King traveling through the mist had come to where Druids and the Maid of the Green Mantle lived, how the King was enchanted, and how the maiden Sheen released him from the enchantment. He told him, too, how the Enchanter was changed into a wolf, and how the wolf carried away Sheen's child. "And the Unique Tale is in part your own history, Flann," said the King of Ireland's Son, "for the child that was left with the Hags of the Long Teeth was no one else than yourself, for you, Flann, have on your breast the stars that denote the Son of a King."

"It is so, it is so," said Flann, "and I will find out what King and Queen were my father and my mother."

"Go to the Hags of the Long Teeth and force them to tell you," said the King's Son.

"I will do that," said Flann, but in his own mind he

said, "I will first bring the Comb of Magnificence to Flame-of-Wine, and I will tell her that I will have to be away for so many years with Mogue and I shall ask her to remember me until I come back to her. Then I shall go to the Hags of the Long Teeth and force them to tell me what King and Queen were my father and mother."

The King of Ireland's Son left Flann to his thoughts and went to find the Gobaun Saor who would clear for him the tarnished blade of the Sword of Light and would show him the way to where the King of the Land of Mist had his dominion.

Mogue spent his time with the ballad singers and the storytellers around the marketstake, and when he came back to his tent he wanted to drink ale and go to sleep, but Flann turned him from the alepot by saying to him, "I want the Comb of Magnificence from you, Mogue."

"By my skin," said Mogue, "it's my blood you'll want next, my lad."

"If you give me the Comb of Magnificence, Mogue, I shall serve you for six years—three years more than I said yesterday. I shall serve you well, even though I am the son of a King and can find out who my father and mother are."

"I won't give you the Comb of Magnificence."

"I'll serve you seven years if you do, Mogue."

Mogue drank and drank out of the alepot, frowning to himself. He put the alepot away and said, "I suppose your life won't be any good to you unless I give you the Comb of Magnificence?"

"That is so, Mogue."

Mogue sighed heavily, but he went to his pack and took out the box that the treasures were in. He let Flann take out the Comb of Magnificence.

"Seven years you will have to serve me," said Mogue, "and you will have to begin your service now."

"I will begin it now," said Flann, but he stole out of the tent, put on his red cloak and went to the King's orchard.

VII

O H, Flann, my treasure-bringer," said Flame-of-Wine, when she came to him. "I have brought you the Comb of Magnificence," said he. Her hands went out and her eyes became large and shining. He put the Comb of Magnificence into her hands.

She put the comb into the back of her hair, and she became at once like the tower that is builded—what broke its height and turned the full sunlight from it has been taken away, and the tower stands, the pride of a King and the delight of a people. When she put the Comb of Magnificence into her hair she became of all Kings' daughters the most stately.

She walked with Flann along the paths of the orchard, but always she was watching her shadow to see if it showed her added magnificence. Her shadow showed nothing. She took Flann to the well in the orchard, and looked down into it, but her image in the well did not show her added magnificence either. Soon she became tired of walking on the orchard paths, and when she

came to the gate she walked no further but stood with
Flann at the gate. "A kiss for you, Flann, my treasure-
bringer," said she, and she kissed him and then went
hurrying away. And as Flann watched her he thought that
although she had kissed him he was not now in her mind.

He went out of the orchard disconsolate, thinking
that when he was on his seven years' service with Mogue
Princess Flame-of-Wine might forget him. As he walked
on he passed the little house where the Spae-Woman had
her besoms and heather-stalks. She ran to him when
she saw him.

"Have you heard that the King's Son has found what
went before, and what comes after the Unique Tale?"
said she.

"That I have. And I have to go to the Hags of the
Long Teeth to find out who my father and mother
were, for surely I am the child who was taken from
Sheen."

"And do you remember that Sheen's seven brothers
were changed into seven wild geese?" said she.

"I remember that, mother."

"And seven wild geese they will be until a maiden
who loves you will give seven drops of her heart's blood
to bring them back to their human shapes."

"I remember that, mother."

"Whatever maid you love, her you must ask if she
would give seven drops of her heart's blood. It may be
that she would. It may be that she would not and that
you would still love her without thought of her giving
one drop of blood of her little finger."

"I cannot ask the maiden I love to give seven drops of her heart's blood."

"Who is the maiden you love?"

"The King's daughter, Flame-of-Wine."

He told the Spae-Woman about the presents he had given her—he told the Spae-Woman too that he had bound himself to seven years' service to Mogue on account of these presents. The Spae-Woman said, "What other treasures are in Mogue's pack?"

"One treasure more—the Girdle of Truth. Whoever puts it on can speak nothing but the truth."

Said the Spae-Woman, "You are to take the Girdle of Truth and give it to Flame-of-Wine. Tell Mogue that I said he is to give it to you without adding one day to your years' service. When Flame-of-Wine has put the girdle around her waist ask her for the seven drops of heart's blood that will bring your mother's seven brothers back to their human shapes. She may love you and yet refuse to give you the seven drops from her heart. But tell her of this, and hear what she will say."

Flann left the Spae-Woman's and went back to Mogue's tent. The loss of his treasures had overcome Mogue and he was drinking steadily and went from one bad temper to another.

"Begin your service now by watching the tent while I sleep," said he.

"There is one thing more I want from you, Mogue," said Flann.

"By the Eye of Balor! You're a cuckoo in my nest. What do you want now?"

"The Girdle of Truth."

"Is it my last treasure you'd be taking on me?"

"The Spae-Woman bid me tell you that you're to give me the Girdle of Truth."

"It's a pity of me, it's a pity of me," said Mogue. But he took the box out of his pack, and let Flann take the girdle.

VIII

FLAME-OF-WINE saw him. She walked slowly down the orchard path so that all might notice the stateliness of her appearance.

"I am glad to see you again, Flann," said she. "Have your comrades yet come back to my father's town?"

Flann told her that one of them had returned.

"Bid him come see me," said Flame-of-Wine. Then she saw the girdle in his hands.

"What is it you have?" said she.

"Something that went with the other treasures—a girdle."

"Will you not let me have it, Flann?" She took the girdle in her hands. "Tell me, youth," she said, "how you got all these treasures?"

"I will have to give seven years' service for them," Flann said.

"Seven years," said she, "but you will remember— will you not—that I loved you for bringing them to me?"

"Will you remember me until I come back from my seven years' service?"

"Oh, yes," said Flame-of-Wine, and she put the girdle around her waist as she spoke.

"Someone said to me," said Flann, "that I should ask the maiden who loved me for seven drops of her heart's blood."

The girdle was now round Flame-of-Wine's waist. She laughed with mockery. "Seven drops of heart's blood," said she. "I would not give this fellow seven eggs out of my robin's nest. I tell him I love him for bringing me the three treasures for a King's daughter. I tell him that, but I should be ashamed of myself if I thought I could have any love for such a fellow."

"Do you tell me the truth now," said Flann.

"The truth, the truth," said she, "of course I tell you the truth. Oh, and there are other truths. I shall be ashamed forever if I tell them. Oh, oh. They are rising to my tongue, and every time I press them back this girdle tightens and tightens until I think it will kill me."

"Farewell, then, Flame-of-Wine."

"Take off the girdle, take off the girdle! What truths are in my mind! I shall speak them and I shall be ashamed. But I shall die in pain if I hold them back. Loosen the girdle, loosen the girdle! Take the rose you gave me and loosen the girdle." She let the rose fall on the ground.

"I will loosen the girdle for you," said Flann.

Flame-of-Wine laughed with mockery.

"But loosen it now. How I have to strive to keep truths back, and oh, what pain I am in! Take the Comb of Magnificence, and loosen the girdle." She threw the comb down on the ground.

He took up the Rose of Sweet Smells and the Comb of Magnificence and he took the girdle of her waist. "Oh, what a terrible thing I put round my waist," said Flame-of-Wine. "Take it away, Flann, take it away. But give me back the Rose of Sweet Smells and the Comb of Magnificence,—give them back to me and I shall love you always."

"You cannot love me. And why should I give seven years in service for your sake? I will leave these treasures back in Mogue's pack."

"Oh, you are a peddler, a peddler. Go from me," said Flame-of-Wine. "And do not be in the Town of the Red Castle tomorrow, or I shall have my father's hunting dogs set upon you." She turned away angrily and went into the Castle.

Flann went back to Mogue's tent and left the Rose of Sweet Smells, the Comb of Magnificence, and the Girdle of Truth upon Mogue's pack. He sat in the corner and cried bitterly. Then the King of Ireland's Son came and told him that his sword was bright once more—that the stains that had blemished its blade had been cleared away by the Gobaun Saor who had also shown him the way to the Land of the Mist. He put his arm about Flann and told him that he was starting now to rescue his love Fedelma from the Castle of the King of the Land of Mist.

THE KING OF THE LAND OF MIST

I

THE King of Ireland's Son came to the place where the river that he followed takes the name of the River of the Broken Towers. It is called by that name because the men of the old days tried to build towers across its course. The towers were built a little way across the river that at this place was tremendously wide.

"The Glashan will carry you across the River of the Broken Towers to the shore of the Land of Mist," the Gobaun Saor had said to the King of Ireland's Son. And now he was at the River of the Broken Towers but the Glashan-creature was not to be seen.

Then he saw the Glashan. He was leaning his back against one of the Towers and smoking a short pipe. The water of the river was up to his knees. He was covered with hair and had a big head with horse's ears. And the Glashan twitched his horse's ears as he smoked in great contentment.

"Glashan, come here," said the King of Ireland's Son.

But the Glashan gave him no heed at all.

"I want you to carry me across the River of the Broken Towers," shouted the King of Ireland's Son.

The Glashan went on smoking and twisting his ears.

And the King of Ireland's Son might have known that the whole clan of the Gruagachs and Glashans are fond of their own ease and will do nothing if they can help it. He twitched his ears more sharply when the King's Son threw a pebble at him. Then after about three hours he came slowly across the river. From his big knees down he had horse's feet.

"Take me on your big shoulders, Glashan," said the King of Ireland's Son, "and carry me across to the shore of the Land of Mist."

"Not carrying any more across," said the Glashan.

The King of Ireland's Son drew the Sword of Light and flashed it.

"Oh, if you have that, you'll have to be carried across," said the Glashan. "But wait until I rest myself."

"What did you do that you should rest?" said the King of Ireland's Son. "Take me on your shoulders and start off."

"Musha," said the Glashan, "aren't you very anxious to lose your life?"

"Take me on your shoulders."

"Well, come then. You're not the first living dead man I carried across." The Glashan put his pipe into his ear. The King of Ireland's Son mounted his shoulders and laid hold of his thick mane. Then the Glashan put his horse's legs into the water and started to cross the River of the Broken Towers.

"The Land of Mist has a King," said the Glashan, when they were in the middle of the river.

"That, Glashan, I know," said the King of Ireland's Son.

"All right," said the Glashan.

Then said he when they were three-quarters of the way across, "Maybe you don't know that the King of the Land of Mist will kill you?"

"Maybe 'tis I who will kill him," said the King of Ireland's Son.

"You'd be a hardy little fellow if you did that," said the Glashan. "But you won't do it."

They went on. The water was up to the Glashan's waist but that gave him no trouble. So broad was the river that they were traveling across it all day. The Glashan threw the King's Son in once when he stooped to pick up an eel.

Said the King of Ireland's Son, "What way is the Castle of the King of the Land of Mist guarded, Glashan?"

"It has seven gates," said the Glashan.

"And how are the gates guarded?"

"I'm tired," said the Glashan, "and I can't talk."

"Tell me, or I'll twist the horse's ears off your head."

"Well, the first gate is guarded by a plover only. It sits on the third pinnacle over the gate, and when anyone comes near it rises up and flies round the Castle crying until its sharp cries put the other guards on the watch."

"And what other guards are there?"

"Oh, I'm tired, and I can talk no more."

The King of Ireland's Son twisted his horse's ears, and then the Glashan said—

"The second gate is guarded by five spearmen."

"And how is the third gate guarded?"

"The third gate is guarded by seven swordsmen."

"And how is the fourth gate guarded?"

"The fourth gate is guarded by the King of the Land of Mist himself."

"And the fifth gate?"

"The fifth gate is guarded by the King of the Land of Mist himself."

"And the sixth gate?"

"The sixth gate is guarded by the King of the Land of Mist."

"And how is the seventh gate guarded?"

"The seventh gate is guarded by a Hag."

"By a Hag only?"

"By a Hag with poisoned nails. But I'm tired now, and I'll talk no more to you. If I could strike a light now I'd smoke a pipe."

Still they went on, and just at the screech of the day they came to the other shore of the River of the Broken Towers. The King of Ireland's Son sprang from the shoulders of the Glashan and went into the mist.

II

HE came to where turrets and pinnacles appeared above the mist. He climbed the rock upon which the Castle was built. He came to the first gate, and as he did the plover that was on the third pinnacle above rose up and flew round the Castle with sharp cries.

He raised a fragment of the ground-rock and flung it against the gate. He burst it open. He dashed in then and through the first courtyard of the Castle.

As he went toward the second gate it was flung open, and the five spearmen ran upon him. But they had not counted on what was to face them—the Sword of Light in the hands of the King of Ireland's Son.

Its stroke cut the spearheads from the spearholds, and its quick glancing dazzled the eyes of the spearmen. On each and every one of them it inflicted the wound of death. He dashed through the second gate and into the third courtyard.

But as he did the third gate was flung open and seven swordsmen came forth. They made themselves like a half circle and came toward the King of Ireland's Son. He dazzled their eyes with a wide sweep of his sword. He darted it swiftly at each of them and on the seven swordsmen too he inflicted wounds of death.

He went through the third courtyard and toward the fourth gate. As he did it opened slowly and a single champion came forth. He closed the gate behind him and stood with a long gray sword in his hand. This was the King of the Land of Mist. His shoulders were where a tall man's head would be. His face was like a stone, and his eyes had never looked except with scorn upon a foe.

When his enemy began his attack the King of Ireland's Son had power to do nothing else but guard himself from that weighty sword. He had the Sword of Light for a guard and well did that bright, swift blade guard him. The two fought across the courtyard making hard places soft and soft places hard with their trampling. They fought from when it was early to when it was noon, and they fought from when it was noon until it was long afternoon. And not a single wound did the King of Ireland's Son inflict upon the King of the Land of Mist, and not a single wound did the King of the Land of Mist inflict upon him.

But the King of Ireland's Son was growing faint and weary. His eyes were worn with watching the strokes and thrusts of the sword that was battling against him. His arms could hardly bear up his own sword. His heart became a stream of blood that would have gushed from his breast.

And then, as he was about to fall down with his head under the sword of the King of the Land of Mist a name rose above all his thoughts—"Fedelma." If he sank down and the sword of the King of the Land of Mist fell on him, never would she be saved. The will became strong again in the King of Ireland's Son. His heart became a steady beating thing. The weight that was upon his arms passed away. Strongly he held the sword in his hand and he began to attack the King of the Land of Mist.

And now he saw that the sword in the hand of his enemy was broken and worn with the guard that the

Sword of Light had put against it. And now he made a strong attack. As the light was leaving the sky and as the darkness was coming down he saw that the strength was waning in the King of the Land of Mist. The sword in his hand was more worn and more broken. At last the blade was only a span from the hilt. As he drew back to the gate of the fourth courtyard the King of Ireland's Son sprang at him and thrust the Sword of Light through his breast. He stood with his face becoming exceedingly terrible. He flung what remained of his sword, and the broken blade struck the foot of the King of Ireland's Son and pierced it. Then the King of the Land of Mist fell down on the ground before the fourth gate.

So weary from his battles, so pained with the wound of his foot was the King of Ireland's Son that he did not try to cross the body and go toward the fifth gate. He turned back. He climbed down the rock and went toward the River of the Broken Towers.

The Glashan was broiling on a hot stone the eel he had taken out of the river. "Wash my wound and give me refreshment, Glashan," said the King of Ireland's Son.

The Glashan washed the wound in his foot and gave him a portion of the broiled eel with cresses and water.

"Tomorrow's dawn I shall go back," said the King of Ireland's Son, "and go through the fifth and sixth and seventh gate and take away Fedelma."

"If the King of the Land of Mist lets you," said the Glashan.

"He is dead," said the King of Ireland's Son, "I thrust my sword through his breast."

"And where is his head?" said the Glashan.

"It is on his corpse," said the King of Ireland's Son.

"Then you will have another fight tomorrow. His life is in his head, and his life will come back to him if you did not cut it off. It is he, I tell you, who will guard the fourth and fifth and sixth gate."

"That I do not believe, Glashan," said the King of Ireland's Son. "There is no one to guard the gates now but the Hag you spoke of. Tomorrow I shall take Fedelma out of her captivity, and we will both leave the Land of Mist. But I must sleep now."

He laid the Sword of Light beside him, stretched himself on the ground and went to sleep. The Glashan drew his horse's legs under him, took the pipe out of his ear, and smoked all through the night.

III

THE King of Ireland's Son rose in the morning but he was in pain and weariness on account of his wounded foot. He ate the cresses and drank the water that the Glashan gave him, and he started off for the Castle of the King of the Mist. "'Tis only an old woman I shall have to deal with today," he said, "and then I shall awaken Fedelma, my love."

He passed through the first gate and the first courtyard, through the second gate and the second courtyard, through the third gate and the third courtyard.

The fourth gate was closed, and as went toward it, it opened slowly, and the King of the Land of Mist stood there—as high, as stone-faced, and as scornful as before, and in his hand he had a weighty gray sword.

They fought as they fought the day before. But the guard the King of Ireland's Son made against the sword of the King of the Land of Mist was weaker than before, because of the pain and weariness that came from his wound. But still he kept the Sword of Light before him and the Sword of the King of the Land of Mist could not pass it. They fought until it was afternoon. The heart in his body seemed turned to a jet of blood that would gush forth. His eyes were straining themselves out of their sockets. His arms could hardly bear up his sword. He fell down upon one knee, but he was able to hold the sword so that it guarded his head.

Then the image of Fedelma appeared before him. He sprang up and his arms regained their power. His heart became steady in his breast. And as he made an attack upon the King of the Land of Mist, he saw that the blade in his hand was broken and worn because of its strokes against the Sword of Light.

They fought with blades that seemed to kindle each other into sparks and flashes of light. They fought until the blade in the hand of the King of the Land of Mist was worn to a hand breadth above the hilt. He drew back toward the gate of the fifth courtyard. The King of Ireland's Son sprang at him and thrust the Sword of Light through his breast. Down on the stones before the fifth gate of his Castle fell the King of the Land of Mist.

The King of Ireland's Son stepped over the body and went toward the fifth gate. Then he remembered what the Glashan had said, "His life is in his head." He went back to where the King of the Land of Mist had fallen. With a clean sweep of his sword he cut the head off the body.

Then out of the mist that was all around three ravens came. With beak and claws they laid hold of the head and lifted it up. They fluttered heavily away, keeping near the ground.

With his sword in his hand the King of Ireland's Son chased the ravens. He followed them through the fourth courtyard, the third courtyard, the second and the first. They flew off the rock on which the Castle was built and disappeared in the mist.

He knew he would have to watch by the body of the King of the Land of Mist, so that the head might not be placed upon it. He sat down before the fifth gate. Pain and weariness, hunger and thirst oppressed him.

He longed for something that would allay his hunger and thirst. But he knew that he could not go to the river to get refreshment of water and cresses from the Glashan.

Something fell beside him in the courtyard. It was a beautiful, bright-colored apple. He went to pick it up, but it rolled away toward the third courtyard. He followed it. Then, as he looked back he saw that the ravens had lighted near the body of the King of the Land of Mist, holding the head in their beaks and claws. He ran back and the ravens lifted the head up again and flew away.

He watched for another long time, and his hunger and his thirst made him long for the bright-colored apple he had seen.

Another apple fell down. He went to pick it up and it rolled away. But now the King of Ireland's Son thought of nothing but that bright-colored apple. He followed it as it rolled.

It rolled through the third courtyard, and the second and the first. It rolled out of the first gate and on to the rock upon which the Castle was built. It rolled off the rock. The King of Ireland's Son sprang down and he saw the apple become a raven's head and beak.

He climbed up the rock and ran back. And when he came into the first courtyard he saw that the three ravens had come back again. They had brought the head to the body, and body and head were now joined. The King of the Land of Mist stood up again, and his head was turned toward his left shoulder. He went to the sixth gate and took up a sword that was beside it.

IV

THEY fought their last battle before the sixth gate. The guard that the King of Ireland's Son made was weak, and if the King of the Land of Mist could have turned fully upon him, he could have disarmed and killed him. But his head had been so placed upon his body that it looked over his left shoulder. He was able to draw his sword down the breast of the King of Ireland's Son, wounding him. The King's Son whirled his sword around his head and flung it at his wry-headed enemy. It swept his head off, and the King of the Land of Mist fell down.

The King of Ireland's Son saw on the outstretched neck the mark of the other beheading. He took up the Sword of Light again and prepared to hold the head against all that might come for it.

But no creature came. And then the hair on the severed head became loose and it was blown away by the wind. And the bones of the head became a powder and the flesh became a froth, and all was blown away by the wind.

Then the King of Ireland's Son went through the sixth courtyard and came to the seventh gate. And before it he saw the last of the sentinels. A Hag, she was seated on the top of a watertank taking white doves out of a basket and throwing them to ravens that flew down from the walls and tore the doves to pieces.

When the Hag saw the King of Ireland's Son she sprang down from the watertank and ran toward him with outstretched arms and long poisoned nails. With a sweep of his sword he cut the nails from her hands. Ravens picked up the nails, and then, as they tried to fly away, they fell dead.

"The Sword of Light will take off your head if you do not take me on the moment to where Fedelma is," said the King of Ireland's Son.

"I am sorry to do it," said the Hag, "but come, since you are the conqueror."

He followed the Hag into the Castle. In a net, hanging across a chamber, he saw Fedelma. She was still, but she breathed. And the branch of hawthorn that put her asleep was fresh beside her. Strands of her bright air came through the meshes of the net and were fastened to the wall. With a sweep of the Sword of Light he cut the strands.

Her eyes opened. She saw the King of Ireland's Son, and the full light came back to her eyes, and the full life into her face.

He cut the net from where it hung and laid it on the ground. He cut open the meshes. Fedelma rose out of it and went into his arms.

He lifted her up and carried her out into the seventh courtyard. Then the Hag who had been one of the sentinels came out of the Castle, closed the door behind her and ran away into the mist, three ravens flying after her.

And as for Fedelma and the King of Ireland's Son, they went through the courtyards of the Castle and through the mists of the country and down to the River of the Broken Towers. They found the Glashan broiling a salmon upon hot stones. Salmon were coming from the sea and the Glashan went in and caught more, broiled and gave them to the King of Ireland's Son and Fedelma to eat. The little black waterhen came out of the river and they fed it. The next day the King of Ireland's Son bade the Glashan take Fedelma on his shoulders and carry her to the other shore of the River of the Broken Towers. And he himself followed the little black waterhen who showed him all the shallow places in the river so that he crossed with the water never above his waist. But he was nearly dead from cold and weariness, and from the wounds on breast and foot when he came to the other side and found the Glashan and Fedelma waiting for him.

They ate salmon again and rested for a day. They bade goodby to the Glashan, who went back to the river to hunt for salmon. Then they went along the bank of the river hand in hand while the King of Ireland's Son told Fedelma of all the things that had happened to him in his search for her.

They came to where the river became known as the River of the Morning Star. And then, in the distance, they saw the Hill of Horns. Toward the Hill of Horns they went, and, at the near side of it, they found a house thatched with the wing of a bird. It was the house of the Little Sage of the Mountain. To the house of the Little Sage of the Mountain Fedelma and the King's Son now went.

THE HOUSE OF CROM DUV

TO THE MEMORY
OF
BEATRICE CASSIDY COLUM

I

THE story is now about Flann. He went through the East gate of the Town of the Red Castle and his journey was to the house of the Hags of the Long Teeth where he might learn what Queen and King were his mother and his father. It is with the youth Flann, once called the Gilly of the Goatskin, that we will go if it be pleasing to you, Son of my Heart. He went his way in the evening, when, as the bard said:—

> The blackbird shakes his metal notes
> Against the edge of day,
> And I am left upon my road
> With one star on my way.

And he went his way in the night, when, as the same bard said:—

> The night has told it to the hills,
> And told the partridge in the nest,
> And left it on the long white roads,
> She will give light instead of rest.

And he went on between the dusk and the dawn, when, as the same bard said again:—

Behold the sky is covered,
As with a mighty shroud:
A forlorn light is lying
Between the earth and cloud.

And he went on in the dawn, when as the bard said
(and this is the last stanza he made, for the King said
there was nothing at all in his adventure) :—

In the silence of the morning
Myself, myself went by,
Where lonely trees sway branches
Against spaces of the sky.

And then, when the sun was looking over the first high
hills he came to a river. He knew it was the river he
followed before, for no other river in the country was
so wide or held so much water. As he had gone with the
flow of the river then he thought he would go against
the flow of the river now, and so he might come back to
the glens and ridges and deep boggy places he had traveled from.

HE met a Fisherman who was drying his nets and he
asked him what name the river had. The Fisherman said it had two names. The people on the right
bank called it the Daybreak River and the people on
the left bank called it the River of the Morning Star.
And the Fisherman told him he was to be careful not
to call it the River of the Morning Star when he was
on the right bank nor the Daybreak River when he was

on the left, as the people on either side wanted to keep
to the name their fathers had for it and were ill-mannered to the stranger who gave it a different name. The
Fisherman told Flann he was sorry he had told him the
two names for the River and that the best thing he
could do was to forget one of the names and call it
just the River of the Morning Star as he was on the
left bank.

Flann went on with the day widening before him
and when the height of the noon was past he came to
the glens and ridges and deep boggy places he had traveled from. He went on with the bright day going before
him and the brown night coming behind him, and at
dusk he came to the black and burnt place where the
Hags of the Long Teeth had their house of stone.

He saw the house with a puff of smoke coming through
every crevice in the stones. He went to the shut door
and knocked on it with the knocking-stone.

"Who's without?" said one of the Hags.

"Who's within?" said Flann.

"The Three Hags of the Long Teeth," said one of
the Hags, "and if you want to know it," said she, "they
are the runners and summoners, the brewers and can-
dlemakers for Crom Duv, the Giant."

Flann struck a heavier blow with the knocking-stone
and the door broke in. He stepped into the smoke-
filled house.

"No welcome to you, whoever you are," said one of
the three Hags who were seated around the fire.

"I am the lad who was called Gilly of the Goatskin, and whom you reared up here," said he, "and I have come back to you."

The three Hags turned from the fire then and screamed at him.

"And what brought you back to us, humpy fellow?" said the first Hag.

"I came back to make you tell me what Queen and King were my mother and father."

"Why should you think a King and Queen were your father and mother?" they said to him.

"Because I have on my breast the stars of a son of a King," said Flann, "and," said he, "I have in my hand a sword that will make you tell me."

He came toward them and they were afraid. Then the first Hag bent her knee to him, and, said she, "Loosen the hearthstone with your sword and you will find a token that will let you know who your father was."

Flann put his sword under the hearthstone and pried it up. But if it were a token, what was under the hearthstone was an evil thing—a cockatrice. It had been hatched out of a serpent's egg by a black cock of nine years. It had the head and crest of a cock and the body of a black serpent. The cockatrice lifted itself up on its tail and looked at him with red eyes. The sight of that head made Flann dizzy and he fell down on the floor. Then it went down and the Hags put the hearthstone above it.

"What will we do with the fellow?" said one of the

Hags, looking at Flann who was in a swoon on the floor.

"Cut off his head with the sword that he threatened us with," said another.

"No," said the third Hag, "Crom Duv the Giant is in want of a servant. Let him take this fellow. Then maybe the Giant will give us what he has promised us for so long—a berry to each of us from the Fairy Rowan Tree that grows in his courtyard."

"Let it be, let it be," said the other Hags. They put green branches on the fire so that Crom Duv would see the smoke and come to the house. In the morning he came. He brought Flann outside, and after a while Flann's senses came back to him. Then the Giant tied a rope round his arms and drove him before him with a long iron spike that he had for a staff.

II

CROM DUV's arms stretched down to his twisted knees; he had long, yellow, overlapping horse's teeth in his mouth, with a fall-down under-lip and a drawn-back upper-lip; he had a matted rug of hair on his head. He was as high as a haystack. He carried in his twisted hand an iron spike pointed at the end. And wherever he was going he went as quickly as a running mule.

He tied Flann's hands behind his back and drew the rope round Flann's body. Then he started off. Flann was dragged on as if at the tail of a cart. Over ditches and through streams; up hillsides and down into hol-

Flann was dragged on.

lows he was hauled. Then they came into a plain as round as the wheel of a cart. Across the plain they went and into a mile-deep wood. Beyond the wood there were buildings—such walls and such heaps of stones Flann never saw before.

But before they had entered the wood they had come to a high grassy mound. And standing on that grassy mound was the most tremendous bull that Flann had ever seen.

"What bull is that, Giant?" said Flann.

"My own bull," said Crom Duv, "the Bull of the Mound. Look back at him, little fellow. If ever you try to escape from my service my Bull of the Mound will toss you into the air and trample you into the ground." Crom Duv blew on a horn that he had across his chest. The Bull of the Mound rushed down the slope snorting. Crom Duv shouted and the bull stood still with his tremendous head bent down.

Flann's heart, I tell you, sank, when he saw the bull that guarded Crom Duv's house. They went through the deep wood then, and came to the gate of the Giant's Keep. Only a chain was across it, and Crom Duv lifted up the chain. The courtyard was filled with cattle— black and red and striped. The Giant tied Flann to a stone pillar. "Are you there, Morag, my byre-maid?" he shouted.

"I am here," said a voice from the byre. More cattle were in the byre and someone was milking them.

There was straw on the ground of the courtyard and

Crom Duv lay down on it and went to sleep with the cattle trampling around him.

A great stone wall was being built all round the Giant's Keep—a wall six feet thick and built as high as twenty feet in some places and in others as high as twelve. The wall was still being built, for heaps of stones and great mixing-pans were about. And just before the door of the Keep was a Rowan Tree that grew to a great height. At the very top of the tree were bunches of red berries. Cats were lying around the stems of the tree and cats were in its branches—great yellow cats. More yellow cats stepped out of the house and came over to him. They looked Flann all over and went back, mewing to each other.

The cattle that were in the courtyard went into the byre one by one as they were called by the voice of the byre-maid. Crom Duv still slept. By and by a little red hen that was picking about the courtyard came near him and holding up her head looked Flann all over.

When the last cow had gone in and the last stream of milk had sounded in the milking-vessel the byre-maid came into the courtyard. Flann thought he would see a long-armed creature like Crom Duv himself. Instead he saw a girl with good and kind eyes, whose disfigurements were that her face was pitted and her hair was bushy. "I am Morag, Crom Duv's byre-maid," said she.

"Will Crom Duv kill me?" said Flann.

"No. He'll make you serve him," said the byre-maid.

"And what will he make me do for him?"

"He will make you help to build his wall. Crom Duv
goes out every morning to bring his cattle to pasture
on the plain. And when he comes back he builds the
wall round his house. He'll make you mix mortar and
carry it to him, for I heard him say he wants a servant
to do that."

"I'll escape from this," said Flann, "and I'll bring
you with me."

"Hush," said Morag, and she pointed to seven yellow
cats that were standing at Crom Duv's door, watching
them. "The cats," said she, "are Crom Duv's watchers
here and the Bull of the Mound is his watcher outside."

"And is this Little Red Hen a watcher too?" said
Flann, for the Little Red Hen was watching them side-
ways.

"The Little Red Hen is my friend and adviser," said
Morag, and she went into the house with two vessels
of milk.

Crom Duv wakened up. He untied Flann and left
him free. "You must mix mortar for me now," he said.
He went into the byre and came out with a great vessel
of milk. He left it down near the mixing-pan. He went
to the side of the house and came back with a trough
of blood.

"What are these for, Crom Duv?" said Flann.

"To mix the mortar with, gilly," said the Giant.
"Bullock's blood and new milk is what I mix my mortar with, so that nothing can break down the walls that

I'm building round the Fairy Rowan Tree. Every day I kill a bullock and every day my byre-maid fills a vessel of milk to mix with my mortar. Set to now, and mix the mortar for me."

Flann brought lime and sand to the mixing-pan and he mixed them in bullock's blood and new milk. He carried stones to Crom Duv. And so he worked until it was dark. Then Crom Duv got down from where he was building and told Flann to go into the house.

The yellow cats were there and Flann counted sixteen of them. Eight more were outside, in the branches or around the stem of the Rowan Tree. Morag came in, bringing a great dish of porridge. Crom Duv took up a wooden spoon and ate porridge out of vessel after vessel of milk. Then he shouted for his beer and Morag brought him vessel after vessel of beer. Crom Duv emptied one after the other. Then he shouted for his knife and when Morag brought it he began to sharpen it, singing a queer song to himself.

"He's sharpening a knife to kill a bullock in the morning," said Morag. "Come now, and I'll give you your supper."

She took him to the kitchen at the back of the house. She gave him porridge and milk and he ate his supper. Then she showed him a ladder to a room above, and he went up there and made a bed for himself. He slept soundly, although he dreamed of the twenty-four yellow cats within, and the tremendous Bull of the Mound outside Crom Duv's Keep.

III

THIS is how the days were spent in the house of Crom Duv. The Giant and his two servants, Flann and Morag, were out of their beds at the mouth of the day. Crom Duv sounded his horn and the Bull of the Mound bellowed an answer. Then he started work on his wall, making Flann carry mortar to him. Morag put down the fire and boiled the pots. Pots of porridge, plates of butter, and pans of milk were on the table when Crom Duv and Flann came in to their breakfasts. Then, when the Giant had driven out his cattle to the pasture Flann cleaned the byre and made the mortar, mixing lime and sand with bullock's blood and new milk. In the afternoon the Giant came back and he and Flann started work on the wall.

All the time the twenty-four yellow cats lay on the branches of the Rowan Tree or walked about the court-yard or lapped up great crocks of milk. Morag's Little Red Hen went hopping round the courtyard. She seemed to be sleepy or to be always considering something. If one of the twenty-four yellow cats looked at her the Little Red Hen would waken up, murmur something, and hop away.

One day the cattle came home without Crom Duv. "He has gone on one of his journeys," said Morag, "and will not be back for a night and a day."

"Then it is time for me to make my escape," said Flann.

"How can you make your escape, my dear, my dear?" said Morag. "If you go by the front the Bull of the Mound will toss you in the air and then trample you into the ground."

"But I have strength and cunning and activity enough to climb the wall at the back."

"But if you climb the wall at the back," said Morag, "you will only come to the Moat of Poisoned Water."

"The Moat of Poisoned Water?"

"The Moat of Poisoned Water," said Morag. "The water poisons the skin of any creature that tries to swim across the Moat."

Flann was downcast when he heard of the Moat of Poisoned Water. But his mind was fixed on climbing the wall. "I may find some way of crossing the poisoned water," he said, "so bake my cake and give me provision for my journey."

Morag baked a cake and put it on the griddle. And when it was baked she wrapped it in a napkin and gave it to him. "Take my blessing with it," said she, "and if you escape, may you meet someone who will be a better help to you than I was. I must keep the twenty-four cats from watching you while you are climbing the wall."

"And how will you do that?" said Flann.

She showed him what she would do. With a piece of glass she made on the wall of the byre the shadows of

flying birds. Birds never flew across the House of Crom
Duv and the cats were greatly taken with the appearances that Morag made with the piece of glass. Six cats
watched, and then another six came, and after them six
more, and after them the six that watched in the Rowan
Tree. And the twenty-four yellow cats sat round and
watched with burning eyes the appearances of birds that
Morag made on the byre-wall. Flann looked back and
saw her seated on a stone, and he thought the Byre-
Maid looked lonesome.

He tried with all his activity, all his cunning, and all
his strength, and at last he climbed the wall at the back
of Crom Duv's house. He gave a whistle to let Morag
know he was over. Then he went through a little wood
and came to the Moat of Poisoned Water.

Very ugly the dead water looked. Ugly stakes stuck
up from the mud to pierce any creature that tried to
leap across. And here and there on the water were
patches of green poison as big as cabbage leaves. Flann
drew back from the Moat. Leap it he could not, and
swim it he dare not.

And just as he drew back he saw a creature he knew
come down to the bank opposite to him. It was Rory
the Fox. Rory carried in his mouth the skin of a calf.
He dropped the skin into the water and pushed it out
before him. Then he got into the water and swam very
cautiously, always pushing the calf's skin before him.
Then Rory climbed up on the bank where Flann was,

and the skin, all green and wrinkled, sank down into the water.

Rory was going to turn tail, but then he recognized Flann. "Master," said he, and he licked the dust on the ground.

"What are you doing here, Rory?" said Flann.

"I won't mind telling you if you promise to tell no other creature," said Rory.

"I won't tell," said Flann.

"Well then," said Rory, "I have moved my little family over here. I was being chased about a good deal, and my little family wasn't safe. So I moved them over here." The fox turned and looked round at the country behind him. "It suits me very well," said he; "no creature would think of crossing this moat after me."

"Well," said Flann, "tell me how you are able to cross it."

"I will," said the fox, "if you promise never to hunt me nor any of my little family."

"I promise," said Flann.

"Well," said Rory, "the water poisons every skin. Now the reason that I pushed the calf's skin across was that it might take the poison out of the water. The water poisons every skin. But where the skin goes the poison is taken out of the water for a while, and a living creature can cross behind it if he is cautious."

"I thank you for showing me the way to cross the moat," said Flann.

"I don't mind showing you," said Rory the Fox, and he went off to his burrow.

There were deerskins and calfskins both sides of the moat. Flann took a calf's skin. He pushed it into the water with a stick. He swam cautiously behind it. When he reached the other side of the moat, the skin, all green and wrinkled, sank in the water.

Flann jumped and laughed and shouted when he found himself in the forest and clear of Crom Duv's house. He went on. It was grand to see the woodpecker hammering on the branch, and to see him stop, busy as he was to say "Pass, friend." Two young deer came out of the depths of the wood. They were too young and too innocent to have anything to tell him, but they bounded alongside of him as he raced along the Hunter's Path. He jumped and he shouted again when he saw the river before him—the river that was called the Daybreak River on the right bank and the River of the Morning Star on the left. He said to himself, "This time, in troth, I will go the whole way with the river. A moving thing is my delight. The river is the most wonderful of all the things I have seen on my travels."

Then he thought he would eat some of the cake that Morag had baked for him. He sat down and broke it. Then as he ate it the thought of Morag came into his mind. He thought he was looking at her putting the cake on the griddle. He went a little way along the river and then he began to feel lonesome. He turned back, "I'll go to Crom Duv's House," said he, "and show Morag the way to escape. And then she and I will follow the river, and I won't be lonesome while she's with me."

So back along the Hunter's Path Flann went. He came to the Moat of Poisoned Water. He found a deerskin and pushed it into the water and then swam cautiously across the moat. He climbed the wall then, and when he put his head above it he saw Morag. She was watching for him.

"Crom Duv has not come back yet," said she, "but oh, my dear, my dear, I can't prevent the yellow cats from watching you come over the wall."

First six cats came and then another six and they sat round and watched Flann come down the wall. They did nothing to him, but when he came down on the ground they followed him wherever he went.

"You crossed the moat," said Morag, "then why did you come back?"

"I came back," said Flann, "to bring you with me."

"But," said she, "I cannot leave Crom Duv's house."

"I'll show you how to cross the moat," said he, "and we'll both be glad to be going by the moving river."

Tears come into Morag's eyes. "I'd go with you, my dear," said she, "but I cannot leave Crom Duv's house until I get what I came for."

"And what did you come for, Morag?" said he.

"I came," said she, "for two of the rowan berries that grow on the Fairy Rowan Tree in Crom Duv's courtyard. I know now that to get these berries is the hardest task in the world. Come within," said she, "and if we sit long enough at the supperboard I will tell you my story."

They sat at the supperboard long, and Morag told—

THE STORY OF MORAG

IV

I WAS reared in the Spae-Woman's house with two other
girls, Baun and Deelish, my foster sisters. The Spae-
Woman's house is on the top of a knowe, away from
every place, and few ever came that way.

One morning I went to the well for water. When I
looked into it I saw, not my own image, but the image
of a young man. I drew up my pitcher filled with water,
and went back to the Spae-Woman's house. At noontide
Baun went to the well for water. She came back and her
pitcher was only half-filled. Before dark Deelish went
to the well. She came back without a pitcher, for it fell
and broke on the flags of the well.

The next day Baun and Deelish each plaited their hair, and they said to her who was foster mother for the three of us: "No one will come to marry us in this far-away place. We will go into the world to seek our fortunes. So," said they, "bake a cake for each of us before the fall of the night."

The Spae-Woman put three cakes on the griddle and baked them. And when they were baked she said to Baun and Deelish: "Will you each take the half of the cake and my blessing, or the whole of the cake without my blessing?" And Baun and Deelish each said, "The whole of the cake will be little enough for our journey."

Each then took her cake under her arm and went the path down the knowe. Then said I to myself, "It would be well to go after my foster sisters for they might meet misfortune on the road." So I said to my foster mother, "Give me the third cake on the griddle until I go after my foster sisters."

"Will you have half of the cake and my blessing or the whole of the cake without my blessing?" said she to me.

"The half of the cake and your blessing, mother," said I.

She cut the cake in two with a black-handled knife and gave me the even half of it. Then said she:—

> May the old sea's
> Seven Daughters—
> They who spin
> Life's longest threads,
> Protect and guard you!

She put salt in my hand then, and put the Little Red Hen under my arm, and I went off.

I went on then till I came in sight of Baun and Deelish. Just as I caught up on them I heard one say to the other, "This ugly, freckled girl will disgrace us if she comes with us." They tied my hands and feet with a rope they found on the road and left me in a wood.

I got the rope off my hands and feet and ran and ran until I came in sight of them again. And when I was coming on them I heard one say to the other, "This ugly, freckled girl will claim relationship with us wherever we go, and we will get no good man to marry us." They laid hold of me again and put me in a lime-kiln, and put beams across it, and put heavy stones on the beams. But my Little Red Hen showed me how to get out of the lime-kiln. Then I ran and I ran until I caught up with Baun and Deelish again.

"Let her come with us this evening," said one to the other, "and tomorrow we'll find some way of getting rid of her."

The night was drawing down now, and we had to look for a house that would give us shelter. We saw a hut far off the road and we went to the broken door. It was the house of the Hags of the Long Teeth. We asked for shelter. They showed us a big bed in the dormer-room, and they told us we could have supper when the porridge was boiled.

The three Hags sat round the fire with their heads

together. Baun and Deelish were in a corner plaiting their hair, but the Little Red Hen murmured that I was to listen to what the Hags said. "We will give them to Crom Duv in the morning," one said. And another said, "I have put a sleeping-pin in the pillow that will be under each, and they will not waken."

When I heard what they said I wanted to think of what we could do to make our escape. I asked Baun to sing to me. She said she would if I washed her feet. I got a basin of water and washed Baun's feet, and while she sang, and while the Hags thought we were not minding them, I considered what we might do to escape. The Hags hung a pot over the fire and the three of them sat around it once more.

When I had washed my foster sister's feet I took a besom and began to sweep the floor of the house. One of the Hags was very pleased to see me doing that. She said I would make a good servant, and after a while she asked me to sit at the fire. I sat in the corner of the chimney. They had put meal in the water, and I began to stir it with a pot stick. Then the Hag that had asked me to the fire said, "I will give you a good share of milk with your porridge if you keep stirring the pot for us." This was just what I wanted to be let do. I sat in the chimney-corner and kept stirring the porridge while the Hags dozed before the fire.

First, I got a dish and ladle and took out of the pot some half-cooked porridge. This I left one side. Then I took down the salt box that was on the chimney shelf and mixed handsful of salt in the porridge left in the pot.

When it was all cooked I emptied it into another dish and brought the two dishes to the table. Then I told the Hags that all was ready. They came over to the table and they gave my foster sisters and myself three porringers of goat's milk. We ate out of the first dish and they ate out of the second. "By my sleep tonight," said one Hag, "this porridge is salty." "Too little salt is in it for my taste," said my foster sister Deelish. "It is as salt as the depths of the sea," said another of the Hags. "My respects to you, ma'am," said Baun, "but I do not taste any salt on it at all." My foster sisters were so earnest that the Hags thought themselves mistaken, and they ate the whole dishful of porridge.

The bed was made for us, and the pillows were laid on the bed, and I knew that the slumber-pin was in each of the pillows. I wanted to put off the time for going to bed so I began to tell stories. Baun and Deelish said it was still young in the night, and that I should tell no short ones, but the long story of Eithne, Balor's daughter. I had just begun that story, when one of the Hags cried out that she was consumed with thirst.

She ran to the pitcher, and there was no water in it. Then another Hag shouted out that the thirst was strangling her. The third one said she could not live another minute without a mouthful of water. She took the pitcher and started for the well. No sooner was she gone than the second Hag said she couldn't wait for the first one to come back, and she started out after her. Then the third one thought that the pair would stay too long talking at the well, and she started after them.

Immediately I took the pillows off our bed and put them on the Hags' bed, taking their pillows instead.

The Hags came back with a half-filled pitcher, and they ordered us to go to our bed. We went, and they sat for a while drinking porringers of water. "Crom Duv will be here the first thing in the morning," I heard one of them say. They put their heads on the pillows and in the turn of a hand they were dead-fast-sound asleep. I told my foster sisters then what I had done and why I had done it. They were very frightened, but seeing the Hags so sound asleep they composed themselves and slept too.

Before the screech of day Crom Duv came to the house. I went outside and saw the Giant. I said I was the servant of the Hags, and that they were sleeping still. He said, "They are my runners and summoners, my brewers, bakers and candle-makers, and they have no right to be sleeping so late." Then he went away.

I knew that the three Hags would slumber until we took the pillows from under their heads. We left them sleeping while we put down a fire and made our breakfast. Then, when we were ready for our journey, we took the pillows from under their heads. The three Hags started up then, but we were out on the door, and had taken the first three steps of our journey.

V

WITHOUT hap or mishap we came at last to the domain of the King of Senlabor. Baun went to sing for the King's foster daughters, and Deelish went to

work at the little loom in the King's chamber. We were
not long at the court of the King of Senlabor when two
youths came there from the court of the King of Ireland—Dermott and Downal were their names. There
was a famous swordsmith with the King of Senlabor and
these two came to learn the trade from him. And my
two foster sisters fell so deeply in love with the two
youths that every night the pillow on each side of me
was wet with their tears.

I went to work in the King's Kitchen. Now the King
had a dish of such fine earthware and with such beautiful patterns upon it that he never let it be carried from
the Kitchen to the Feast-Hall, nor from the Feast-Hall
to the Kitchen without going himself behind the servant
who carried it. One day the servant brought it into the
Kitchen to be washed and the King came behind the
servant. I took the dish and cleaned it with thrice-
boiled water and dried it with cloths of three different
kinds. Then I covered it with sweet-smelling herbs and
left it in a bin where it was sunk in soft bran. The King
was pleased to see the good care I took of his dish, and
he said before his servant that he would do me any
favor I would ask. There and then I told him about my
two foster sisters Baun and Deelish, and how they were
in love with the two youths Dermott and Downal who
had come from the court of the King of Ireland. I asked
that when these two youths were being given wives, that
the King should remember my foster sisters.

The King was greatly vexed at my request. He declared that the two youths had on their breasts the stars

that denoted the sons of Kings and that he intended they should marry his own two foster daughters when the maidens were of age to wed. "It may be," he said, "that these two youths will bring what my Queen longs for—a berry from the Fairy Rowan Tree that is guarded by the Giant Crom Duv."

The next day the King's Councillor was feeding the birds and I was sifting the corn. I asked him what was the history of the Fairy Rowan Tree that the Giant Crom Duv guarded and why it was that the Queen longed for a berry of it. There and then he told me this story:—

THE STORY OF THE FAIRY ROWAN TREE

THE history of the Fairy Rowan Tree (said the King's Councillor), begins with Ainé, the daughter of Mananaun who is Lord of the Sea. Curoi, the King of the Munster Fairies loved Ainé and sought her in marriage. But the desire of the girl's heart was set upon Fergus who was a mortal, and one of the Fianna of Ireland. Now when Mananaun MaeLir heard Curoi's proposals and learned how his daughter's heart was inclined, he said, "Let the matter be settled in this way: we will call a hurling-match between the Fairies of Munster and the Fianna of Ireland with Curoi to captain one side and Fergus to captain the other, and if the Fairies win, Ainé will marry Curoi and if the Fianna have the victory she will have my leave to marry this mortal Fergus."

· 235 ·

So a hurling-match was called for the first day of Lunassa, and it was to be played along the strand of the sea. Mananaun himself set the goal-marks, and Ainé was there to watch the game. It was played from the rising of the sun until the high tide of noon, and neither side won a goal. Then the players stopped to eat the refreshment that Mananaun had provided.

This is what Mananaun had brought from his own country, Silver-Cloud Plain: a branch of bright-red rowan berries. Whoever ate one of these rowan berries his hunger and his weariness left him in a moment. The berries were to be eaten by the players, Mananaun said, and not one of them was to be taken into the world of the mortals or the world of the Fairies.

When they stopped playing at the high tide of noon the mortal Fergus saw Ainé and saw her for the first time. A spirit that he had never felt before flowed into him at the sight of Mananaun's daughter. He forgot to eat the berry he was given and held it in his mouth by the stalk.

He went into the hurling-match again and now he was like a hawk amongst small birds. Curoi defended the goal and drove the ball back. Fergus drove it to the goal again; the two champions met and Curoi's hurl, made out of rhinoceros' horn, did not beat down Fergus's hurl made out of the ash of the wood. The hosts stood aside and left the game to Fergus and Curoi. Curoi's hurl jerked the ball upward; then Fergus gave it the double stroke—first with the handle and then with the weighted end of the hurl and drove it, beautifully as a flying bird, between the goal marks that Mananaun had set up. The match was won by the goal that Fergus had gained.

The Fianna then invited the Fairies of Munster to a feast that they were giving to Fergus and his bride. The Fairies went, and Mananaun and Ainé went before them all. Fergus marched at the head of his troop with the rowan berry still hanging from his mouth. And as he went he bit the stalk and the berry fell to the ground. Fergus never heeded that.

When the feast was over he went to where Mananaun stood with his daughter. Ainé gave him her hand. "And it is well," said Conan, the Fool of the Fianna, "that this thick-witted Fergus has at last dropped the berry out of his mouth." "What berry?" said Curoi, who was standing by. "The rowan berry," said Conan, "that he carried across two townlands the same as if he were a bird."

When Mananaun heard this he asked about the berry that Fergus had carried. It was not to be found. Then the Fianna and the Fairies of Munster started back to look for a trace of it. What they found was a wonderful Rowan Tree. It had grown out of the berry that Fergus had let fall, but as yet there were no berries on its branches.

Mananaun, when he saw the tree said, "No mortal may take a berry that grows on it. Hear my sentence now. Fergus will have to guard this tree until he gets one who will guard it for him. And he may not see nor keep company with Ainé his bride until he finds one who will guard it better than he can guard it himself." Then Mananaun wrapped his draughter in his cloak and strode away in a mist. The Fairy Host went in one direction and the Fianna in another, and Fergus was left standing sorrowfully by the Fairy Rowan Tree.

Next day (said Morag), when the King's Councillor was feeding the birds and I was sifting the corn, he told me the rest of the history of the Fairy Rowan Tree. Fergus thought and thought how he might leave off watching it and be with Ainé, his bride. At last he bethought him of a Giant who lived on a rocky island with only a flock of goats for his possessions. This Giant had begged Finn, the Chief of the Fianna, for a strip of the land of Ireland, even if it were only the breadth of a bull's hide. Finn had refused him. But now Fergus sent to Finn and asked him to bring the Giant to be the guardian of the Fairy Rowan Tree and to give him the land around it. "I mislike letting this giant Crom Duv have any portion of the land of Ireland," said Finn, "nevertheless we cannot refuse Fergus."

So Finn sent some of the Fianna to the Giant and they found him living on a bare rock of an island with only a flock of goats for his possessions. Crom Duv lay on his back and laughed when he heard what message the men of the Fianna brought to him. Then he put them and his flock of goats into his big boat and rowed them over to Ireland.

Crom Duv swore by his flock of goats he would guard the Fairy Rowan Tree until the red berries ceased to come on its branches. Fergus left his place at the tree then and went to Aine, and it may be that she and he are still together.

Well did Crom Duv guard the tree, never going far from it and sleeping at night in its branches. And one year a heifer came and fed with his flock of goats and another year a bullock came. And these were the beginning of his great herd of cattle. He has become more and more greedy for cattle, said the King's Councillor, and now he takes them away to far pastures. But still the Fairy Rowan Tree is well guarded. The Bull that is called the Bull of the Mound is on guard near by, and twenty-four fierce yellow cats watch the tree night and day.

The Queen of Senlabor and many another woman besides desires a berry from the Fairy Rowan Tree that stands in Crom Duv's courtyard. For the woman who is old and who eats a berry from that tree becomes young again, and the maid who is young and who eats a berry gets all the beauty that should be hers of right. And now, my maid, said the King's Councillor to me, I have told you the history of the Fairy Rowan Tree.

When I heard all this (said Morag), I made up my mind to get a berry for the Queen and maybe another berry besides from the Fairy Rowan Tree in Crom Duv's courtyard. When the King came into the kitchen again, I asked him would he permit my foster sisters to marry

Downal and Dermott if I brought to his Queen a berry from the Fairy Rowan Tree. He said he would give permission heartily. That night when I felt the tears of Baun and Deelish I told them I was going to search for such a dowry for them that when they had it the King would let them marry the youths they had set their hearts on. They did not believe I could do anything to help them, but they gave me leave to go.

The next day I told the Queen I was going to seek for a berry from the Fairy Rowan Tree. She told me that if I could bring back one berry to her she would give me all the things she possessed. I said goodby to my foster sisters and with the Little Red Hen under my arm I went toward the house of the Hags of the Long Teeth. I built a shelter and waited till Crom Duv came that way. One early morning he came by. I stood before him and I told him that I wanted to take service in his house.

Crom Duv had never had a servant in his house. But I told him that he should have a byre-maid and that I was well fitted to look after his cattle. He told me to follow him. I saw the Bull of the Mound and I was made wonder how I could get away with the berry from the Fairy Rowan Tree. Then I saw the twenty-four fierce yellow cats and I was made wonder how I could get the berry from the tree. And after that I found out about the Moat of Poisoned Water that is behind the high wall at the back of Crom Duv's house. And so now (said Morag), you know why I have come here and how hard the task is I have taken on myself.

VI

Now that he had heard the history of the Fairy Rowan Tree, Flann often looked at the clusters of scarlet berries that were high up on its branches. The Tree could be climbed, Flann knew. But on the top of the tree and along its branches were the fierce yellow cats —the cats that the Hags of the Long Teeth had reared for Crom Duv, thinking that he would some time give each of them the berry that would make them young again. And at the butt of the tree there were more cats. And all about the courtyard the Hags' fierce cats paraded themselves.

The walls round the Giant's Keep were being built higher by Crom Duv, helped by his servant Flann. The Giant's herd was now increased by many calves, and Morag the byre-maid had much to do to keep all the cows milked. And day and night Morag and Flann heard the bellowing of the Bull of the Mound.

Now one day while Crom Duv was away with his herd, Flann and Morag were in the courtyard. They saw the Little Red Hen rouse herself up, shake her wings and turn a bright eye on them. "What dost thou say, my Little Red Hen?" said Morag.

"The Pooka," murmured the Little Red Hen. "The Pooka rides a fierce horse, but the Pooka himself is a timid little fellow." Then the Little Red Hen drooped her wings again, and went on picking in the courtyard.

"The Pooka rides a fierce horse," said Morag, "if

the Pooka rides a fierce horse he might carry us past the Bull of the Mound."

"And if the Pooka himself is a timid little fellow we might take the fierce horse from him," said Flann.

"But this does not tell us how to get the berries off the Fairy Rowan Tree," said Morag.

"No," said Flann, "it does not tell us how to get the berries off the tree the cats guard."

The next day Morag gave grains to the Little Red Hen and begged for words. After a while the Little Red Hen murmured, "There are things I know, and things I don't know, but I do know what grows near the ground, and if you pull a certain herb, and put it round the necks of the cats they will not be able to see in the light nor in the dark. And tomorrow is the day of Sowain," said the Little Red Hen. She said no more words. She had become sleepy and now she flew down and roosted under the table. There she went on murmuring to herself —as all hens murmur—where the Children of Dana hid their treasures—they know, for it was the Children of Dana who brought the hens to Ireland.

"Tomorrow," said Morag to Flann, "follow the Little Red Hen, and if she makes any sign when she touches an herb that grows near the ground, pluck that herb and bring it to me."

That night Morag and Flann talked about the Pooka and his fierce horse. On Sowain night—the night before the real short days begin—the Pooka rides through the countryside touching any fruit that remains, so that it may bring no taste into winter. The blackberries that were good to eat the day before are no good on November day, because the Pooka touched them the night before. What else the Pooka does no one really knows. He is a timid fellow as the Little Red Hen said, and he hopes that the sight of his big black horse and the sound of its trampling and panting as he rides by will frighten people out of his way, for he has a great fear of being seen.

The next day the Little Red Hen stayed in the courtyard until Crom Duv left with his herd. Flann followed her. She went here and there between the house and the wall at the back, now picking a grain of sand and now an ant or spider or fly. And as she went about the Little Red Hen murmured a song to herself:—

> When sleep would settle on me
> Like the wild bird down on the nest,
> The wind comes out of the West:
> It tears at the door, maybe,
> And frightens away my rest—
> When sleep would come upon me
> Like the wild bird down on the nest.
>
> The cock is aloft with his crest:
> The barn-owl comes from her quest
> She fixes an eye upon me
> And frightens away my rest
> When sleep would settle on me
> Like the wild bird down on its nest.

Flann watched all the Little Red Hen did. He saw her

put her head on one side and look down for a while at a certain herb that grew near the ground. Flann plucked that herb and brought it to Morag.

The cattle had come home, but Crom Duv was not with them. Morag milked the cows and brought all the milk within, leaving no milk for the cats to drink outside. Six came into the kitchen to get their supper there. One after another they sprang up on the table, one more proud and overbearing than the other. Each cat ate without condescending to make a single mew. "Cat of my heart," said Morag to the first, when he had finished drinking his milk. "Cat of my heart! How noble you would look with this red around your neck." She held out a little satchel in which a bit of the herb was sewn. The first cat gave a look that said, "Well, you may put it on me." Morag put the red satchel around his neck and he jumped off the table.

It was so with all the other cats. They finished lapping their milk and Morag showed them the red ribbon satchel. They let her put it round each of their necks and then they sprang off the table, and marched off more scornful and overbearing than before.

Six of the fierce yellow cats climbed into the branches of the Fairy Rowan Tree; six stayed in the kitchen; six went into Crom Duv's chamber, and six went to march round the house, three taking each side. No sound came from the cats that were within or without. Morag drew a ball of cotton across the floor, and the cats that were in the kitchen gave no sign of seeing it. "The sight has left their eyes," said Morag. "Then," said Flann, "I will climb the Fairy Rowan Tree and bring down two berries." "Be sure you bring down two, my dear, my dear," said Morag.

They went out to the courtyard and Flann began to climb the Fairy Rowan Tree with all suppleness, strength, and cunning. The cats that were below felt him going up the tree and the cats that were above humped themselves up. Flann passed the first branch on which a cat was crouched. He went above where the rowan berries were, and bending down he picked two of them and put them into his mouth.

He came down quickly with the cats tearing at him. Others had come out of the house and were mewing and spitting in the courtyard. Only one had fastened itself on Flann's jerkin, and this one would not let go. "Come into the wood, come into the wood," said Morag. "Now we must stand between the house and the mound, and wait till the Pooka rides by." Flann put the two berries into her hand, they jumped across the chain, and ran from the house of the Giant Crom Duv.

VII

THEY went into the wood, Flann and Morag, and the Little Red Hen was under Morag's arm. They thought they would hide behind trees until they heard the coming of the Pooka and his horse. But they were not far in the wood when they heard Crom Duv coming toward his house. He came toward them with the iron spike in his hand. Flann and Morag ran. Then from tree to tree Crom Duv chased them, shouting and snorting and smashing down branches with the iron spike in his hand. Morag and Flann came to a stream, and as they ran along its bank they heard the trampling and panting of a horse coming toward them. Up it came, a great black horse with a sweeping mane. "Halt, Pooka," said Flann in a commanding voice. The black horse halted and the Pooka that was its rider slipped down to its tail.

Flann held the snorting horse and Morag got on its back. Then Flann sprang up between Morag and the horse's head. Crom Duv was just beside them. "Away, Pooka, away," said Flann, and the horse started through the wood like the wind of March.

And then Crom Duv blew on the horn that was across his breast and the Bull of the Mound bellowed in answer. As they went by the mound the Bull charged down and its horns tossed the tail of the Pooka's horse. The Bull turned and swept after them with his head down and hot breath coming out of his nostrils. And when they were in the hollow he was on the height, and when they were on the height he was in the hollow. And a hollow or a height behind his Bull came Crom Duv himself.

Then the breath of the Bull became hot upon Morag and Flann and the Pooka. "Oh, what shall we do now?"

*Up it came, a great black horse
with a sweeping mane.*

said Morag to the Pooka who was hanging on to the horse's tail, his little face all twisted up with fear.

"Put your hand into my horse's ear and fling behind what you will find there," said the Pooka, his teeth chattering. Flann put his hand into the horse's right ear and found a twig of ash. He flung it behind them. Instantly a tangled wood sprang up. They heard the Bull driving through the tangle of the wood and they heard Crom Duv shouting as he smashed his way through the brakes and branches. But the Bull and the man got through the wood and again they began to gain on the Pooka's horse. Again the breath of the Bull became hot upon them. "Oh, Pooka, what shall we do now?" said Morag.

"Put your hand into my horse's ear and fling behind what you will find there," said the Pooka, his teeth chattering with fear as he held on to his horse's tail. Flann put his hand into the horse's left ear and he found a bubble of water. He flung it behind them. Instantly it spread out as a lake and as they rode on, the lake waters spread behind them.

Morag and Flann never knew whether the Giant and the Bull went into that lake, or if they did, whether they ever came out of it. They crossed the river that marked the bounds of Crom Duv's domain and they were safe. Flann pulled up the horse and jumped on to the ground. Morag sprang down with the Little Red Hen. Then the Pooka swung forward and whispered into his horse's ear. Instantly it struck fire out of its hooves and sprang down the side of a hill. From that day to this Morag and Flann never saw sight of the Pooka and his big, black, snorting and foaming horse.

"Dost thou know where we are, my Little Red Hen?" said Morag when the sun was in the sky again.

"There are things I know and things I don't know," said the Little Red Hen, "but I know we are near the place we started from."

"Which way do we go to come to that place, my Little Red Hen?" said Morag.

"The way of the sun," said the Little Red Hen. So Morag and Flann went the way of the sun and the Little Red Hen hopped beside them. Morag had in a weaselskin purse around her neck the two rowan berries that Flann had given her.

They went toward the house of the Spae-Woman. And as they went Morag told Flann of the life she had there when she and her foster sisters were growing up, and Flann told Morag of the things he did when he was in the house of the Spae-Woman after she and her foster sisters had left it.

They climbed the heather-covered knowe on which was the Spae-Woman's house and the Little Red Hen went flitting and fluttering toward the gate. The Spae-Woman's old goat was standing in the yard, and its horns went down and its beard touched its knees and it looked at the Little Red Hen. Then the Little Red Hen flew up on its back. "We're here again, here again," said the Little Red Hen.

And then the Spae-Woman came to the door and saw who the comers were. She covered them with kisses and watered them with tears, and dried them with cloths silken and with the hair of her head.

VIII

FLANN told the Spae-Woman all his adventures. And when he had told her all he said—"What Queen is my mother, O my fosterer?"

"Your mother," said the Spae-Woman, "is Caintigern, the Queen of the King of Ireland."

"And is my mother then not Sheen whose story has been told me?"

"Her name was changed to Caintigern when her husband who was called the Hunter-King made himself King over Ireland and began to rule as King Connal."

"Then who is my comrade who is called the King of Ireland's Son?"

"He too is King Connal's son, born of a queen who died at his birth and who was wife to King Connal before he went on his wanderings and met Sheen your mother."

And as the Spae-Woman said this someone came and stood at the doorway. A girl she was and wherever the sun was it shone on her, and wherever the breeze was it rippled over her. White as the snow upon a lake frozen over was the girl, and as beautiful as flowers and as alive as birds were her eyes, while her cheeks had the red of fox-gloves and her hair was the blending of five bright soft colors. She looked at Flann happily and her eyes had the kind look that was always in Morag's eyes. And she came and knelt down, putting her hands on his knees.

"I am Morag, Flann," she said.

"Morag indeed," said he, "but how have you become so fair?"

"I have eaten the berry from the Fairy Rowan Tree," said she, "and now I am as fair as I should be."

All day they were together and Flann was happy that his friend was so beautiful and that so beautiful a being was his friend. And he told her of his adventures in the Town of the Red Castle and of the Princess Flame-of-Wine and his love for her. "And if you love her still I will never see you again," said Morag.

"But," said Flann, "I could not love her after the way she mocked at me."

"When did she mock at you?"

"When I took her a message that the Spae-Woman told me to give her."

"And what was that message?"

" 'Ask her,' said the Spae-Woman, 'for seven drops of her heart's blood—she can give them and live—so that the spell may be taken from the seven wild geese and the mother who longs for you may be at peace again.' This was the message the Spae-Woman told me to give Flame-of-Wine. And though I had given her wonderful gifts she laughed at me when I took it to her. And by the way she laughed I knew she was hard of heart."

"Yet seven drops of heart's blood are hard to give," said Morag sadly.

"But the maiden who loves can give them," said the Spae-Woman who was behind.

"It is true, foster mother," said Morag.

That evening Morag said, "Tomorrow I must prepare for my journey to the Queen of Senlabor. You, Flann, may not come with me. The Spae-Woman has sent a message to your mother, and you must be here to meet her when she comes. A happy meeting to her and you, O Flann of my heart. And I shall leave you a token to give to her. So tomorrow I go to the Queen of Senlabor with the Rowan Berry and I shall bring my Little Red Hen for company, and shall stay only until my sisters are wed to Dermott and Downal, your brothers."

The next day when he came into the house he saw Morag dressed for her journey but seated at the fire. She was pale and ill-looking. "Do not go today, Morag," said he. "I shall go today," said Morag. She put her hand into the bosom of her dress and took out a newly woven handkerchief folded. "This is a token for your mother," she said. "I have woven it for her. Give her this gift from me when you have welcomed her."

"That I will do, Morag, my heart," said Flann.

The Spae-Woman came in and kissed Morag goodby and said the charm for a journey over her.

> May my Silver-
> Shielded Magian
> Shed all lights
> Across your path.

Then Morag put the Little Red Hen under her arm and started out. "I shall find you," said she to Flann, "at the Castle of the King of Ireland, for it is there I shall go when I part from my foster sisters and the Queen of Senlabor. Kiss me now. But if you kiss anyone until you kiss me again you will forget me. Remember that."

"I will remember," said Flann, and he kissed Morag and said, "When you come to the King of Ireland's Castle we will be married."

"You gave me the Rowan Berry," said Morag, "and the Rowan Berry gave me all the beauty that should be mine. But what good will my beauty be to me if you forget me?"

"But, Morag," said he, "how could I forget you?"

She said nothing but went down the side of the knowe and Flann watched and watched until his eyes had no power to see any more.

THE SPAE-WOMAN

I

THERE are many things to tell you still, my kind foster child, but little time have I to tell you them, for the barnacle-geese are flying over the house, and when they have all flown by I shall have no more to say. And I have to tell you yet how the King of Ireland's Son won home with Fedelma, the Enchanter's daughter, and how it came to pass that the Seven Wild Geese that were Caintigern's brothers were disenchanted and became men again. But above all I have to tell you the end of that story that was begun in the house of the Giant Crom Duv—the story of Flann and Morag.

The barnacle-geese are flying over the house as I said. And so they were crossing and flying on the night the King of Ireland's Son and Fedelma whom he had brought from the Land of Mist stayed in the house of the Little Sage of the Mountain. On that night the Little Sage told them from what bird had come the wing that thatched his house. That was a wonderful story. And he told them too about the next place they should go to —the Spae-Woman's house. There, he said he would find people that they knew—Flann, the King's Son's comrade, and Caintigern, the wife of the King of Ireland, and Fedelma's sister, Gilveen.

In the morning the Little Sage of the Mountain took them down the hillside to the place where Fedelma and the King's Son would get a horse to ride to the Spae-Woman's house. The Little Sage told them from what people the Spae-Woman came and why she lived amongst the poor and foolish without name or splendor or riches. And that, too, was a wonderful story.

Now as the three went along the riverside they saw a girl on the other side of the river and she was walking from the place toward which they were going. The girl sang to herself as she went along, and the King's Son and Fedelma and the Little Sage of the Mountain heard what she sang,—

A berry, a berry, a red rowan berry,
A red rowan berry brought me beauty and love.

But drops of my heart's blood, drops of my heart's blood,
Seven drops of my heart's blood I have given away.

Seven wild geese were men, seven wild geese were men,
Seven drops of my heart's blood are there for your spell.

A kiss for my love, a kiss for my love,
May his kiss go to none till he meet me again.

If to one go his kiss, if to one go his kiss,
He may meet, he may meet, and not know me again.

The girl on the other bank of the river passed on, and the King's Son and Fedelma with the Little Sage of the Mountain came to the meadow where the horse was. A heavy, slow-moving horse he seemed. But when they mounted him they found he had the three qualities of Finn's steeds—a quick rush against a hill, the gait of a fox, easy and proud, on the level ground, and the jump of a deer over barriers. They left health and good luck with the Little Sage of the Mountain, and on the horse he gave them they rode on to the Spae-Woman's house.

II

WHEN Fedelma and the King of Ireland's Son came to the Spae-Woman's house, who was the first person they saw there but Gilveen, Fedelma's sister!

She came to where they reined their horse and smiled in the faces of her sister and the King of Ireland's Son. And she it was who gave them their first welcome. "And you will be asking how I came here," said Gilveen, "and I will tell you without wasting candle-light. Myself and sister Aefa went to the court of the King of Ireland after you, my sister, had gone from us with the lucky man of your choice. And as for Aefa, she has been lucky too in finding a match and she is now married to Maravaun the King's Councillor. I have been with Caintigern the Queen. And now the

Queen is in the house of the Spae-Woman with the youth Flann and she is longing to give the clasp of welcome to both of you. And if you sit beside me on this grassy ditch I will tell you the whole story from the first to the last syllable."

Tl.ey sat together, and Gilveen told Fedelma and the King's Son the story. The Spae-Woman had sent a message to Caintigern the Queen to tell her she had tidings of her first-born son. Thereupon Caintigern went to the Spae-Woman's house and Gilveen, her attendant, went with her. She found there Flann who had been known as Gilly of the Goatskin, and knew him for the son who had been stolen from her when he was born. Flann gave his mother a token which had been given him by a young woman. The token was a handkerchief and it held seven drops of heart's blood. The Spae-Woman told the Queen that these seven drops would disenchant her brothers who had been changed from their own forms into the forms of seven wild geese.

And while Gilveen was telling them all this Flann came to see whose horse was there, and great was his joy to find his comrade the King of Ireland's Son. They knew now that they were the sons of the one father, and they embraced each other as brothers. And Flann took the hand of Fedelma and he told her and the King's Son of his love for Morag. But when he was speaking of Morag, Gilveen went away.

Then Flann took them into the Spae-Woman's house,

and the Queen who was seated at the fire rose up and
gave them the clasp of welcome. The face she turned
to the King's Son was kindly and she called him by
his child's name. She said too that she was well pleased
that he and Flann her son were good comrades, and
she prayed they would be good comrades always.

Fedelma and the King of Ireland's Son rested themselves for a day. Then the Spae-Woman said that the
Queen would strive on the next night—it was the night
of the full moon—to bring back her seven brothers to
their own forms. The Spae-Woman said too that the
Queen and herself should be left alone in the house
and that the King of Ireland's Son with Flann and
Fedelma and Gilveen should go toward the King of
Ireland's Castle with MacStairn the woodman, and
wait for the Queen at a place a day's journey away.

So the King of Ireland's Son and Flann, Fedelma
and Gilveen bade goodby to the Queen, to the Spae-
Woman, and to the Spae-Woman's house, and started
their journey toward the King's Castle with Mac-
Stairn the Woodman who walked beside their horses,
a big axe in his hands.

At night MacStairn built two bothies for them—
one covered with green boughs for Fedelma and
Gilveen and one covered with cut sods for Flann and
the King of Ireland's Son. Flann lay near the opening
of this bothie. And at night, when the only stir in the
forest was that of the leaves whispering to the Secret

People, Gilveen arose from where she lay and came to the other bothie and whispered Flann's name. He awakened, and thinking that Morag had come back to him (he had been dreaming of her), he put out his arms, drew Gilveen to him and kissed her. Then Gilveen ran back to her own bothie. And Flann did not know whether he had awakened or whether he had remained in a dream.

But when he arose the next morning no thought of Morag was in his mind. And when the King's Son rode with Fedelma he rode with Gilveen. Afterwards Gilveen gave him a drink that enchanted him, so that he thought of her night and day.

Neither Fedelma nor the King's Son knew what had come over Flann. They mentioned the name he had spoken of so often—Morag's name—but it seemed as if it had no meaning for him. At noon they halted to bide until the Queen came with or without her seven brothers. Flann and Gilveen were always together. And always Gilveen was smiling.

III

WHEN Caintigern had come, when she knew her son Flann, and when it was known to her and to the Spae-Woman that the token Morag had given him held the seven drops of heart's blood that would bring back to their own forms the seven wild geese that were Caintigern's brothers—when all this was

known the Spae-Woman sent her most secret messenger
to the marshes to give word to the seven wild geese
that they were to fly to her house on the night when
the moon was full. Her messenger was the corncrake.
She traveled night and day, running swiftly through
the meadows. She hid on the edge of the marshes and
craked out her message to the seven wild geese. At last
they heard what she said. On the day before the night
of the full moon, they flew, the seven together, toward
the Spae-Woman's house.

No one was in the house but Caintigern the Queen.
The door was left open to the light of the moon. The
seven wild geese flew down and stayed outside the door,
moving their heads and wings in the full moonlight.

Then Caintigern arose and took bread that the
Spae-Woman had made. She moistened it in her
mouth, and into each bit of moistened bread she put
a piece of the handkerchief that had a drop of blood.
She held out her hand, giving each the moistened
bread. The first that ate it fell forward on the floor of
the Spae-Woman's house, his head down on the
ground. His sister saw him then as a kneeling man
with his arms held behind him as if they were bound.
And when she looked outside she saw the others like
kneeling men with their heads bent and their arms
held behind them. Then Caintigern said, giving the
Spae-Woman her secret name, "O Grania Oi, let it be
that my brothers be changed back to men!" When she
said this she saw the Spae-Woman coming across the

courtyard. The Spae-Woman waved her hands over the bent figures. They lifted themselves up as men— as naked, gray men.

The Spae-Woman gave each a garment and the seven men came into the house. They would stand and not sit, and for long they had no speech. Their sister knelt before each and wet his hand with her tears. She thought she should see them as youths or as young men, and they were gray now and past the prime of their lives.

They stayed at the house and speech came back to them. Then they longed to go back to their father's, but Caintigern could not bear that they should go from her sight. At last four of her brothers went and three stayed with her. They would go to her husband's Castle and the others would go too after they had been at their father's. Then one day Caintigern said farewell. The thanks that was due to the Spae-Woman, she said she would give by her treatment of the maid who had given the token to her son Flann. And she prayed that Morag would soon come to the King's Castle.

She went with her three brothers to the place where Flann and the King of Ireland's Son, Fedelma and Gilveen waited for them. A smith groomed and decked horses for all of them and they rode toward the King of Ireland's Castle, MacStairn, the Woodman, going before to announce their coming.

The King of Ireland waited at the stone where the riders to his Castle dismount, and his steward, his Councillor, and his Druid were beside him. He lifted his wife off her horse and she brought him to Flann. And when the King looked into Flann's eyes he knew he was his son and the son of Sheen, now known as Caintigern. He gave Flann a father's clasp of welcome. And the queen brought him to her own three brothers who had been estranged from human companionship from before he knew her. And she brought him to the youth who was always known as the King of Ireland's Son, and him his father welcomed from the path of danger.

And then the King's Son took Fedelma to his father and told him she was his love and his wife to be. And the King welcomed Fedelma to the Castle.

Then said Gilveen, "There is a secret between this young man, Flann, and myself."

"What is the secret?" said the Queen, laying her hands suddenly upon Gilveen's shoulders.

"That I am his wife to be," said Gilveen.

The Queen went to her son and said, "Dost thou not remember Morag, Flann, who gave the token that thou gavest me?"

And Flann said, "Morag! I think the Spae-Woman spoke of her name in a story."

"I am Flann's wife to be," said Gilveen, smiling in his face.

"Yes, my wife to be," said Flann.

Then the King welcomed Gilveen too, and they all went into the Castle. He told his wife he had messages from the King of Senlabor about his other sons Dermott and Downal, saying that they were making good names for themselves, and that everything they did was becoming to sons of Kings. In the hall Fedelma saw Aefa her other sister. Aefa was so proud of herself since she married Maravaun the King's Councillor that she would hardly speak to anyone. She gave her sisters the tips of her fingers and she bowed very slightingly to the two youths. The King questioned his Druid as to when it would be well to have marriages made in his Castle and the Druid said it would be well not to make them until the next appearance of the full moon.

IV

As for Morag she went by track and path, by boher and bohereen, through fords in rivers and over stepping-stones across them, until at last she came to the country of Senlabor and to the Castle of the King.

No one of high degree was in the Castle, for all had gone to watch the young horses being broken in the meadow by the river; the King and Queen had gone, and the King's foster daughters; and of the maids in the Castle, Baun and Deelish had gone too. The King's Councillor also had gone from the Castle. Morag went and stayed in the kitchen, and the maids who were there did not know her, either because they were new and had not heard her spoken of at all, or because she had changed to such beauty through eating the berry of the Fairy Rowan Tree that no one could know her now for Morag who had cleaned dishes in that kitchen before.

It was Breas the King's Steward who came to her and asked her who she was. She told him. Then Breas looked sharply at her and saw she was indeed Morag who had been in the King's kitchen. Then he said loudly, "Before you left you broke the dish that the King looked on as his especial treasure, and for this, you will be left in the Stone House. I who have power in this matter order that it be so." Then he said in her ear, "But kisses and sweet words would make me willing to save you."

Morag, in a voice raised, called him by that evil name that he was known by to the servants and their gossips. But the servants, hearing that name said in the hearing of Breas, pretended to be scandalized. They went to Morag and struck her with the besoms they had for sweeping the floor.

Just then her foster sisters, Baun and Deelish, came into the kitchen. Seeing her there they knew her. They spoke to her quietly, but with anger, saying they had not wanted her to go on the journey she had taken, but, as she had gone it was a pity she had come back, for now she had behaved in an ill-mannered way, and they who were her foster sisters would be thought to be as ill-mannered; they told her too that before she came back they were well-liked by all, and that Breas had even ordered a shady place to be given them at the horse-breaking sports, and they had been able to see the two youths who had broken the horses, Dermott and Downal.

"It was for a benefit to you that I came back," said Morag. "I shall ask one of you to do a thing for me. You, Baun, sing for the foster daughters of the King. Before they sleep tonight ask them to tell the Queen that Morag has returned, and has a thing to give her."

"I shall try to remember that, Morag," said Baun.

Morag was taken to the Stone House by strong-armed bondswomen, and Baun and Deelish sat in corners and cried and did not go near her.

That night the King's foster daughters kept awake for long, and after Baun had sung to them they asked her to tell them what had happened in the Castle. Then Baun remembered the tumult in the kitchen that had come from the name given to Breas. She told the King's foster daughters that Morag had come back. "She was reared in the same house with us," said Baun, "but she is not of the same parents." And then she said; "If your Fair Finenesses can remember, tell the Queen that Morag has come back."

The next day when they were walking with the Queen one of the King's foster daughters said, "Did you know of a maid named Morag? I have heard that she has been away and has come back."

"How did she fare?" said the Queen.

"We have not heard that," said the maiden who spoke.

The Queen went to where Baun and Deelish were and from them she heard that Morag had been put into the Stone House on the charge that she had broken the King's dish when she had been in the Castle before. Now the Queen knew that the dish had been safe after Morag had left. She went to the King's Steward and accused him of having broken it and Breas admitted that it was so. Thereupon he lost his rank and became the meanest and the most despised servant in the Castle.

The Queen went to the Stone House and took Morag out. She asked her how she had fared and thereupon Morag put the Rowan Berry in the Queen's hand. She hastened to her own chamber and ate it, and her youth and beauty came back to her, and the King who had grown solitary, loved the Queen again.

Then Morag came to great honor in the Castle and the Queen asked her to name the greatest favor she could think of. And the favor that Morag named was marriages for her foster sisters with the two youths they loved, Downal and Dermott from the court of the King of Ireland.

The Queen, when she heard this, brought fine clothes out of her chests and gave them to Baun and Deelish. When they had dressed in these clothes the Queen made them known to the two youths. Downal and Dermott fell in love with Morag's foster sisters, and the King named a day for the pairs to marry.

Morag waited to see the marriages, and the King and Queen made it a grand affair. There were seven hundred guests at the short table, eight hundred at the long table, nine hundred at the round table, and a thousand in the great hall. I was there, and I heard the whole story. But I got no present save shoes of paper and stockings of butter-milk and these a herdsman stole from me as I crossed the mountains.

But Morag got better presents, for the Queen gave her three gifts—a scissors that cut cloth of itself, a ball of thread that went into the needle of itself, and a needle that sewed of itself.

V

M ORAG, with the three gifts that the Queen of Senlabor gave her, came again to the Spae-Woman's house. Her Little Red Hen was in the court-yard, and she fluttered up to meet her. But there was no sign of any other life about the place. Then, below at the washing-stream she found the Spae-Woman rinsing clothes. She was standing on the middle-stones, clapping her hands as if in great trouble. "Oh, Morag, my daughter Morag," cried the Spae-Woman, "there are signs on the clothes—there are signs on the clothes!"

After a while she ceased crying and clapping her

hands and came up from the stream. She showed
Morag that in all the shifts and dimities she washed
for her, a hole came just above where her heart would
be. Morag grew pale when she saw that, but she stood
steadily and she did not wail. "Should I go to the
King's Castle, fosterer?" said she. "No," said the Spae-
Woman, "but to the woodman's hut that is near the
King's Castle. And take your Little Red Hen with
you, my daughter," said she, "and do not forget the
three presents that the Queen of Senlabor gave you."
Then the Spae-Woman stood up and said the blessing
of the journey over Morag:—

> May the Olden
> One, whom Fairy
> Women nurtured
> Through seven ages,
> Bring you seven
> Waves of fortune.

Morag gave her the clasp of farewell then, and went on
her way with the Little Red Hen under her arm and
the three presents that the Queen of Senlabor gave
her in her pouch.

Morag was going and ever going from the blink of
day to the mouth of dark and that for three crossings
of the sun, and at last she came within sight of the
Castle of the King of Ireland. She asked a dog-boy for
the hut of MacStairn the Woodman and the hut was
shown to her. She went to it and saw the wife of Mac-

Stairn. She told her she was a girl traveling alone and she asked for shelter. "I can give you shelter," said MacStairn's wife, "and I can get you earnings too, for there is much sewing-work to be done at this time." Morag asked her what reason there was for that, and the woodman's wife told her there were two couples in the Castle to be married soon. "One is the youth whom we have always called the King of Ireland's Son. He is to be married to a maiden called Fedelma. The other is a youth who is the King's son too, but who has been away for a long time. Flann is his name. And he is to be married to a damsel called Gilveen."

When she heard that, it was as if a knife had been put into and turned in her heart. She let the Little Red Hen drop from her arm. "I would sew the garments that the damsel Gilveen is to wear," said she, and she sat down on the stone outside the woodman's hut. MacStairn's wife then sent to the Castle to say that there was one in her hut who could sew all the garments that Gilveen would send her.

The next day, with a servant walking behind, Gilveen came to the woodman's hut with a basket of cloths and patterns. The basket was left down and Gilveen began to tell MacStairn's wife how she wanted them cut, stitched, and embroidered. Morag took up the crimson cloth and let her scissors—the scissors that the Queen of Senlabor gave her—run through it. It cut out the pattern exactly. "What a wonderful scissors," said Gilveen. She stooped down to where Morag was sitting on the stone outside of the woodman's house and took up the scissors in her hand. She examined it. "I cannot give it back to you," said she. "Give it to me, and I will let you have any favor you ask." "Since you want me to ask you for a favor," said Morag, "I ask that you let me sit at the supper table tonight alone with the youth you are to marry." "That will do me no harm," said Gilveen. She went away, taking the scissors and smiling to herself.

That night Morag went into the Castle and came to the supper table where Flann was seated alone. But Gilveen had put a sleeping-draught into Flann's cup and he neither saw nor knew Morag when she sat at the table. "Do you remember, Flann," said she, "how we used to sit at the supperboard in the house of Crom Duv?" But Flann did not hear her, nor see her, and then Morag had to go away.

VI

THE next day Gilveen came to where Morag sat on the stone outside the woodman's hut to watch her stitch the garment she had cut out. The thread went into the needle of itself. "What a wonderful ball of thread," said Gilveen, taking it up. "I cannot give it back to you. Ask me for a favor in place of it." "Since you would have me ask a favor," said Morag, "I ask that you let me sit at the supper table alone with the youth you are going to marry." "That will do me no harm," said Gilveen. She took the ball of thread and went away smiling.

That night Morag went into the Castle and came to the supper table where Flann was seated alone. But Gilveen again had put a sleeping-draught into his cup, and Flann did not see or know Morag. "Do you not remember, Flann," said she, "the story of Morag that I told you across the supperboard in the House of Crom Duv?" But Flann gave no sign of knowing her, and then Morag had to go away.

The next day Gilveen came to watch Morag make the red embroideries upon the white garment. When she put the needle into the cloth it worked out the pattern of itself. "This is the most wonderful thing of all," said Gilveen. She stooped down and took the needle in her hand. "I cannot give this back to you," she said, "and you will have to ask for a favor that will recompense you." "If I must ask for a favor," said Morag, "the only favor I would ask is that you let me sit at the supper table tonight alone with the youth you are to marry." "That will do me no harm," said Gilveen, and she took the needle and went away smiling.

Morag went to the Castle again that night, but this time she took the Little Red Hen with her. She scattered grains on the table and the Little Red Hen picked them up. "Little Hen, Little Red Hen," said Morag, "he slept too when I gave the seven drops of my heart's blood for his mother's sake." The Little

Red Hen flew into Flann's face. "Seven drops of heart's blood, seven drops of heart's blood," said the Little Red Hen, and Flann heard the words.

He opened his eyes and saw the Little Red Hen on the table and knew that she belonged to one that he had known. Morag, at the other side of the table, looked strange and shadowy to him. But he threw crumbs on the table and fed the Little Red Hen, and as he watched her picking up the crumbs the memory of Morag came back to him. Then he saw her. He knew her for his sweetheart and his promised wife and he went to her and asked her how it came that she had not been in his mind for so long. "I will tell you how you came to forget me," said she, "it was because of the kiss you gave Gilveen, and the enchantment she was able to put on you because of that kiss."

There was sorrow on Morag's face when she said that, but the sorrow went as the thin clouds go from before the face of the high-hung moon, and Flann saw her as his kind comrade of Crom Duv's and as his beautiful friend of the Spae-Woman's house. They kissed each other then, and every enchantment went but the lasting enchantment of love, and they sat with hands joined until the log in the fire beside them had burnt itself down into a brand and the brand had burnt itself into ashes, and all the time that passed was, as they thought, only while the watching-gilly outside walked from one side of the Castle Gate to the other.

Gilveen had come into the room and she saw Flann and Morag give each other a true-lover's kiss. She went away. But the next day she came to the King's Steward, Art, who at one time wanted to marry her, and whom she had refused because Aefa, her sister, had married one of a higher degree—she came to Art and she told him that she would not marry Flann because she had found out that he had a low-born sweetheart. "And I am ready to marry you, Art," she said. And Art was well pleased, and he and Gilveen left the Castle to be married.

Then the day came when Fedelma and the King of Ireland's Son, and Morag and Flann were married. They were plighted to each other in the Circle of Stones by the Druids who invoked upon them the powers of the Sun, the Moon, the Earth, and the Air. They were married at the height of the day and they feasted at night when the wax candles were lighted round the tables. They had Greek honey and Lochlinn beer; ducks from Achill, apples from Emain, and venison from the Hunting Hill; they had trout and grouse and plovers' eggs and a boar's head for every King in the company. And these were the Kings who sat down to table with the King of Eirinn: the King of Sorcha, the King of Hispania, the King of Lochlinn, and the King of the Green Island who had Sunbeam for his daughter. And they had there the best heroes of Lochlinn, the best storytellers of Alba, the best bards of Eirinn. They laid sorrow and they raised music, and the harpers played until the great champion Split-the-Shields told a tale of the realm of Greece and how he slew the three lions that guarded the daughter of the King. They feasted for six days and the last day was better than the first, and the laugh they laughed when Witless, the Saxon fool, told how Split-the-Shields' story should have ended, shook the young jackdaws out of every chimney in the Castle and brought them down fluttering on the floors.

The King of Ireland lived long, but he died while his sons were in their strong manhood, and after he passed away the Island of Destiny came under the equal rule of the two. And one had rule over the courts and cities, the harbors and the military encampments. And the other had rule over the waste places and the villages and the roads where masterless men walked. And the deeds of one are in the histories the shanachies have written in the language of the learned, and the deeds of the other are in the stories the people tell to you and to me.

> *When I crossed the Ford*
> *They were turning the Mountain Pass;*
> *When I stood on the Steppingstones*
> *They were travelling the Road of Glass.*

THE END